Disney DESCENDANTS

MAL'S

~~Maleficent's~~

SPELL BOOK

DISNEY PRESS

Los Angeles • New York

Printed in the United States of America

First Edition, July 2015

5 7 9 10 8 6 4

FAC-008598-15282

Library of Congress Control Number: 2014960191

ISBN 978-1-4847-2638-9

For more Disney Press fun, visit www.disneybooks.com

Visit DisneyDescendants.com

SUSTAINABLE FORESTRY INITIATIVE

Certified Sourcing

www.sfiprogram.org

SFI-00993

This Label Applies to Text Stock Only

MAL'S ~~Maleficent's~~ SPELL BOOK

ADAPTED BY TINA McLEEF

BASED ON THE FILM BY
JOSANN McGIBBON & SARA PARRIOTT

DISNEP PRESS
Los Angeles • New York

MAGICAL ITEMS

Amulet of Health

Bead of Force

Boots of Levitation

Boots of Speed

Broom of Flying

Candle of Truth

MALEFICENT'S SPELL BOOK,
AKA THE VILLAINS' KIDS'
NONE-OF-YOUR-BUSINESS BOOK.

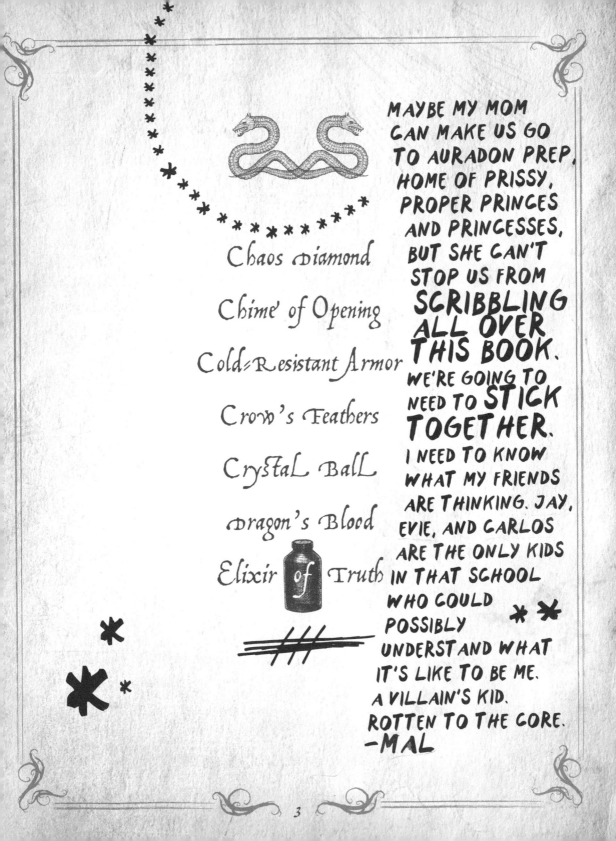

Chaos Diamond

Chime of Opening

Cold-Resistant Armor

Crow's Feathers

Crystal Ball

Dragon's Blood

Elixir of Truth

MAYBE MY MOM CAN MAKE US GO TO AURADON PREP, HOME OF PRISSY, PROPER PRINCES AND PRINCESSES, BUT SHE CAN'T STOP US FROM **SCRIBBLING ALL OVER THIS BOOK.** WE'RE GOING TO NEED TO **STICK TOGETHER.** I NEED TO KNOW WHAT MY FRIENDS ARE THINKING. JAY, EVIE, AND CARLOS ARE THE ONLY KIDS IN THAT SCHOOL WHO COULD POSSIBLY UNDERSTAND WHAT IT'S LIKE TO BE ME. A VILLAIN'S KID. ROTTEN TO THE CORE. —MAL

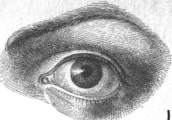

Elixir of Vision

Eye of Newt

Fairy Wings

Force Field Ring

Harp of Charming

Hat of Disguise

Magic Wand

I'M DIRTY, NO GOOD DOWN TO THE BONE, YOUR WORST NIGHTMARE, CAN'T TAKE ME HOME

JAY HERE. I NORMALLY WOULDN'T SAY THIS, BUT I'M GOING TO MISS THE ISLE OF THE LOST. LIKE I'M NOT GOING TO BE LYING AROUND CRYING ABOUT IT OR ANYTHING, BUT I KIND OF LIKE OUR DAYS NOW, RUNNING THROUGH THE DIRTY STREETS, JUMPING ROOFTOP TO ROOFTOP, CUTTING SCHOOL. I STOLE TWO CELL PHONES AND A WHOLE PILE OF CANDY BARS FROM THE CORNER STORE TODAY. HOW'S THAT FOR FUN?

Princess Evie was here

So I got some mischief
In my blood
Can you blame me?
I never got no love

Medallion of Thought Projection

Rapier of Puncturing

Rubies

You didn't have to write that it was you, Jay. We can all tell *Rhino Hide* by your terrible handwriting.
xoxo Evie

Scepter

Scrying Bowl

Trident of Warning

WHAT AM I SUPPOSED TO BE WRITING IN THIS THING? LIKE MY THOUGHTS AND STUFF? OKAY... HERE GOES...

THEY THINK I'M CALLOUS, A LOW-LIFE HOOD I FEEL SO USELESS, MISUNDERSTOOD.

—CARLOS

BUUUUUUUURN. MY PENMANSHIP! YOU REALLY HIT ME WHERE IT HURTS, EVIE!

MAL WANTS US TO CONFESS ALL OF OUR FEELINGS TO THIS BOOK. TIME TO GET REAL DEEP AND STUFF GUYS.

CAT HAIR

It is a known fact

That witches acquire and maintain

Cats not for their company,

But for their hair.

The fur can be used in a variety

Of Stews and even potions.

Odorless and tasteless,

The hair increases the potency

Of whatever substance it is mixed into.

I'm glad I never eat at your house, Mal. Cat hair in stew?!? GROSS!

OH PLEEEEEASE, GUYS. I JUST WANT US TO STAY CONNECTED WHEN WE GET TO AURADON. THOSE PRINCES AND PRINCESSES ARE KNOWN FOR TRYING TO DRIVE WEDGES BETWEEN VILLAINS. WE HAVE TO BE ON GUARD AT ALL TIMES. NO TALKING TO THEM TOO MUCH. NO HANGING OUT WITH THEM TOO MUCH. THEY DON'T CALL THEM PRINCE CHARMINGS FOR NOTHING.

I liked that, Carlos. IT WAS REAL.

Something I shouldn't admit:
I think you're the sweetest of all of us.

HE IS, I'LL GIVE
YOU THAT.

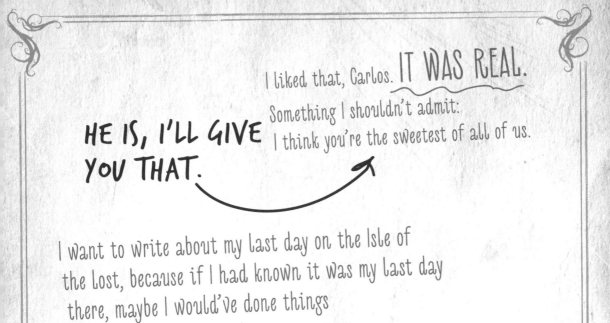

I want to write about my last day on the Isle of
the Lost, because if I had known it was my last day
there, maybe I would've done things
differently. I had a stale
croissant for breakfast,
took a nap, and then
met up with you
guys. Then I saw Mal taking candy from that baby.
That's when it all went down.

SOUNDS LIKE A PERFECT DAY TO ME.
WHAT DO YOU MEAN, YOU "WOULD'VE
DONE THINGS DIFFERENTLY"?

I probably would've hung out in my studio sewing and designing—just
doing what I LOVE. Maybe my mom and I would've made poison apples.
Maybe I would've hitched a ride on the back of one of the dump trucks
in town. You never know. . . .

Removing a Hex

An enemy's hex Can set everything off course,
Can cause pain, Weakness, and even paralysis.
To thwart it, One must reflect the curse
At the sender.

INSTRUCTIONS

Set a magic mirror
In a bowL of black salt.
Across from it, set an object
That represents the sender:
A photo or a belonging of theirs.

Let stand for ten days.

Hope we won't have to use this in Auradon. I don't think princes and princesses even know how to put hexes on people, right?

PROBABLY NOT. MAL, I COULDN'T BELIEVE YOUR FACE WHEN MALEFICENT SHOWED UP IN THE MARKET THIS MORNING. AND I THOUGHT MY MOM WAS SCARY.

Yeah . . . it's not exactly fun to be lectured in front of all your friends about the difference between being mean and being evil. That's all I've heard my entire life: THINK BIG, MAL. LONG LIVE EVIL. WHY CAN'T YOU BE MORE LIKE ME?

WHAT'S THE DEAL WITH US GOING TO AURADON PREP, ANYWAY? SOME PRINCE DECLARED THIS? I DON'T DO UNIFORMS UNLESS THEY'RE <u>LEATHER</u>.

Yes, Belle and the Beast's son—a preppy prince named Ben—declared that the children of the Isle of the Lost deserve a chance to live on Auradon. What was he thinking?! My mom has a plan, I'm sure. There's no way she wants us to go there and just twiddle our thumbs.

MY MOM'S MASTER PLAN FOR EVIL

1) MAL, EVIE, JAY, AND CARLOS WILL ARRIVE AT AURADON PREP AND START LOOKING FOR THE FAIRY GODMOTHER'S MAGIC WAND.

2) WHEN WE LOCATE THE MAGIC WAND, WE WILL STEAL IT AND RETURN TO THE ISLE OF THE LOST.

3) AS SOON AS MALEFICENT HAS BOTH HER SCEPTER AND THE FAIRY GODMOTHER'S MAGIC WAND, SHE WILL BE ABLE TO BEND BOTH GOOD AND EVIL TO HER WILL.

4) THE SPELL CAST ON THE ISLE OF THE LOST WILL BE BROKEN. VILLAINS WILL BE FREE TO LEAVE THE ISLAND FOR THE FIRST TIME IN DECADES.

5) TOGETHER WE WILL OVERTAKE AURADON AND RECLAIM IT AS OUR OWN.

~~Owls~~ DOGS

Owls are known as

Harbingers of death.

When encountering one,
RUFF RUFFF!!

Never look directly into GRRRRRRRR!!!!

The creature's eyes.

WAIT... NO NO NO
NO NO. THERE ARE
DOGS ON
AURADON?!?! THOSE
VICIOUS, SCARY
BEASTS THAT
RUN AROUND
IN PACKS,
TEARING PEOPLE
APART
WITH THEIR
RAZOR-SHARP
TEETH? HOW AM
I SUPPOSED TO
GO THERE NOW?

WET LITTLE NOSE

Do not let its ~~talons~~ graze

Your uncovered skin.

Any contact can bring

Cut it out,
Jay. Carlos—
you'll be fine!
No dogs will
rip you apart,
at least not
on my watch.
XO

Sudden, often tragic, circumstances.

Luck Spell

Fortune, fame, and power lies
In the mystery of the skies.
The stars, the moon, burning bright,
Light up the longest, darkest night.

Stand beneath this blackened dome
No more than ten paces from your home.
Then hold your palms up toward the east
And repeat these words after a harvest feast:

BRING ME LUCK,

THE EASE OF LIVING,

OPPORTUNITY, AND PROSPERITY.

We have to use this one as soon as we get there and our magic works. I'll need it to find that prince my mom was talking about. She's, like, obsessed with the idea of me marrying one of the princes and having my own little happily ever after. I can't say it's not kind of appealing. . . .

DON'T FORGET THE MIRRORS. SHE REQUESTED THE MOTHER-IN-LAW SUITE HAVE LOTS OF MIRRORS.

Haha, oh right.

Auradon Pros

— I won't have to fluff my mom's furs.
— I won't have to scrape off my mom's bunions.
— I won't have to touch up her gray roots

Auradon Cons

— Dogs
— We'll be outcasts.
— Dogs
— We have to actually go to school and pretend we like it.
— DOGS
— DOGS

∽ EVIE'S GUIDE TO GUYS ∽

- ∽ DO look your best at royal balls and other events where you might meet a prince.

- ∽ DO select a prince who is tall, with clear skin and huge, bright eyes (blue preferred).

- ∽ DO take into account how much land the prince has and whether he will inherit a castle.

- ∽ DO think about how big his castle is compared to others in the land.

- ∽ DO compliment a prince when he is wearing royal regalia: he is sure to take pride in his family name.

- ∽ DON'T ask too many questions. Let the prince tell you about himself.

- ∽ DON'T seem too eager. Play it cool.

- ∽ DON'T mention you are a villain's kid until after your first date (whenever possible).

**Come on, Evie, I just ate. . . .
Do you want me to LOSE MY LUNCH?**

Every Princess Has to Kiss Some "Frogs" to Find Her Prince

Three-Legged Frogs

Three-legged frogs may appear
During a full moon
By a business or house that will
Soon receive financial rewards.
If you see one, do not touch or harm the frog,
Or a curse may unintentionally be put
Upon you.

RIBBIT RIBBIT RIBBIT

← RIBBIT RIBBIT

RIBBIT RIBBIT

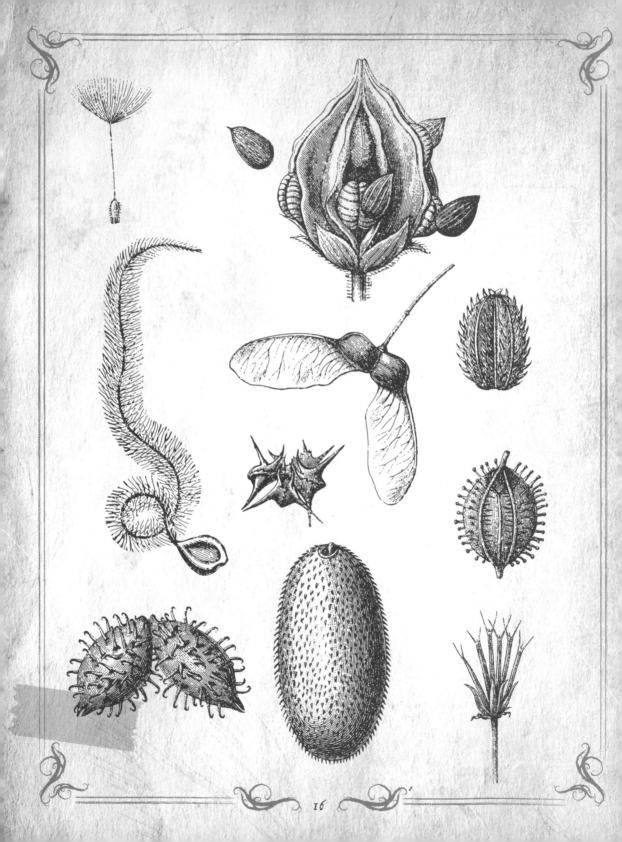

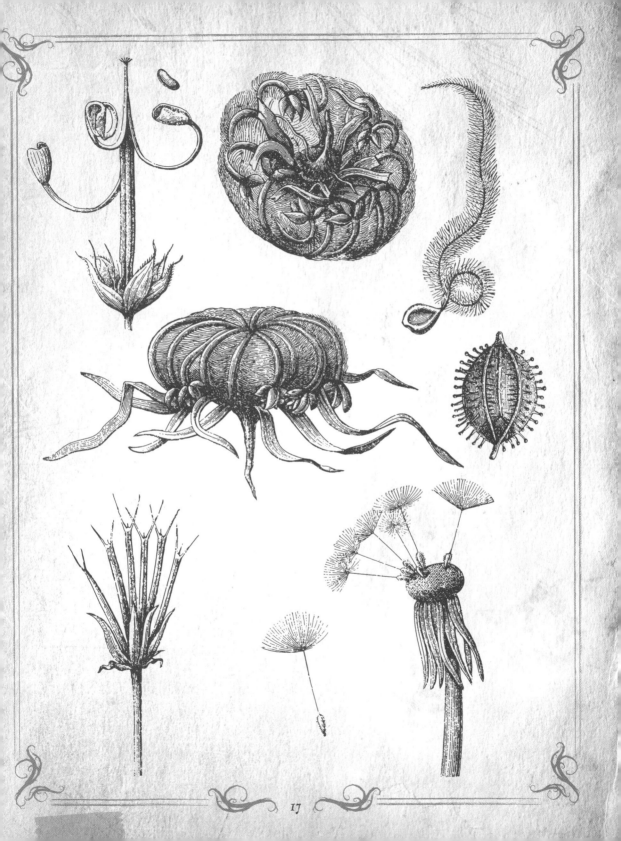

A Chant for Wisdom

BRING ME THE WISDOM OF ALL THOSE

Who came before me—
Their clarity of thought,
Their determined purpose.

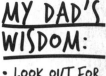

MY DAD'S WISDOM:

- LOOK OUT FOR YOURSELF AND NO ONE ELSE.

BRING ME THE WISDOM OF ALL THOSE

Who came before me—
Their clarity of thought,
Their determined purpose.

- BEWARE OF GENIES BEARING GIFTS.

- THREE STOLEN WATCHES ARE BETTER THAN ONE BOUGHT

BRING ME THE WISDOM OF ALL THOSE FROM A VENDOR.

Who came before me—
Their clarity of thought,
Their determined purpose.

- IF ANYONE ASKS WHERE THE MERCHANDISE CAME FROM, SAY IT "FELL OFF A TRUCK." HA HA HAAA!!!!

Your dad seemed like he was going to genuinely miss you, Jay.
  Maybe that's just because he needs you to steal stuff for his store,
but still. Did you hear my mom? She just kept going on about me
meeting princes and then how I needed to fix my eyebrows before
I left for Auradon.

At least she gave us
her magic mirror. We
can use it to find
the Fairy Godmother's
magic wand.

Who knew that little tiny mirror she always used to apply
lipstick was a MAGIC mirror? With crazy MAGIC powers and
the ability to find anything anywhere? Not me.

AURADON PREP IS GOING TO BE TORTURE. I KNOW, BUT SHE SAID IT'LL HELP ME BEING EXCITED ABOUT ONE SMALL THING. WHEN MY MOM GAVE ME THIS SPELL BOOK FOR THE FIRST TIME EVER, I'LL BE ABLE TO USE SPELLS, REVERSE CURSES, AND MIX POTIONS IN AURADON. EVEN I HAVE TO ADMIT ... THAT'S KIND OF COOL, RIGHT? BEING MAGIC WILL ACTUALLY WORK IN AURADON.

Totally cool. You can admit it.

FIRST WE TAKE OVER AURADON PREP, THEN AURADON ...
THEN THE WORLD!

Snake Eggs

Eating (snake eggs)

REPULSIVE! YOUR MOM LIKES EATING BABY PYTHONS?!?

Has been known to restore strength,

Increase vitality,

And sharpen the senses.

IS THAT A YO MAMA JOKE?!

Python eggs are most delectable.

It is best to eat them cold

Just hours before they hatch.

I KNOW WE HAVE TO LEAVE FOR AURADON SOON, BUT I'M
FEELING A LITTLE—I DON'T KNOW . . . WEIRD, OKAY? IT'S
JUST THAT MY WHOLE LIFE IT'S ALWAYS BEEN ME AND MY
DAD. US TWO AGAINST THE WORLD. SINCE I WAS A KID,
I'VE BEEN LIFTING CELL PHONES FOR HIM TO SELL IN HIS
SHOP OR PICKING THE POCKETS OF EVERY CUSTOMER THAT
WALKED THROUGH THE DOOR. *THERE'S NO TEAM IN I,*
HE'D TELL ME. BUT THAT'S THE THING: WE'VE ALWAYS
BEEN A TEAM, OUR OWN LITTLE TWO-PERSON TEAM,
JUST ME AND HIM. IT'LL JUST BE WEIRD TO BE ALONE IN
AURADON . . . YOU KNOW?

You won't be alone,
Jay. We'll be there
for you. Our own
little FOUR-person
team now.

RIGHT. JUST REMEMBER:
THERE'S NO TEAM IN I.

Whatever.

Smudging

Smudging is a powerful way
To cleanse a person, place, or object
Of negative energy.

SAGE, CEDAR, OR SWEETGRASS

ARE BEST FOR THIS PROCESS.

Place bundle in a clay bowl and light one end.
Let the smoke rise around you.
Bring it over your head to cleanse your thoughts.
Pass objects through it to purify them.

This is our first entry from a stretch limo. When it arrived
this morning to take us to Auradon Prep, I was like WHOA.
Talk about showing up in style.

It's stocked with every type of candy, and Jay's already dismantled the TV and stereo so they're now "portable." We're zipping through the Isle of the Lost, making our way to the border, and I'm already picturing what life on Auradon will be like. If this is at all a preview, there are fancy balls and evening gowns and butlers with coattails in my future. Glasses of sparkling cider served on silver trays.

WE GET IT, IT'S GOING TO BE AWESOME.

THAT WAS INSANE! WE WERE SPEEDING TOWARD THE EDGE OF THE ISLE OF THE LOST, RIGHT WHERE THE ISLAND ENDS AND IS SURROUNDED BY WATER. THEN THE DRIVER REACHED UP AND HIT THIS BUTTON ON THE REMOTE, AND I WASN'T SURE IF THE LIMO WAS GOING TO CRASH INTO THE WATER, OR HE WAS GOING TO BLOW US UP OR WHAT . . . BUT THEN . . . BAM! OUT OF NOWHERE THIS BRIDGE APPEARED. WE DROVE RIGHT OVER IT AND INTO AURADON. SERIOUSLY, GUYS, WAS THAT NOT THE COOLEST THING YOU'VE EVER SEEN?!?!

I don't know about the coolest . . . but it was pretty cool.

YEAH, YOU WERE SCARED OUT OF YOUR MIND, I COULD TELL. YOU WERE HOLDING ME SO TIGHT I COULD BARELY BREATHE. I THINK I STILL HAVE HAND MARKS ON MY NECK.

CARLOS THE Ladybug

Ladybugs showing up in one's life
Foretell a time of luck and protection
When wishes start to become actualized.

Worries will disperse when a ladybug appears
As they shield us from our aggravations.

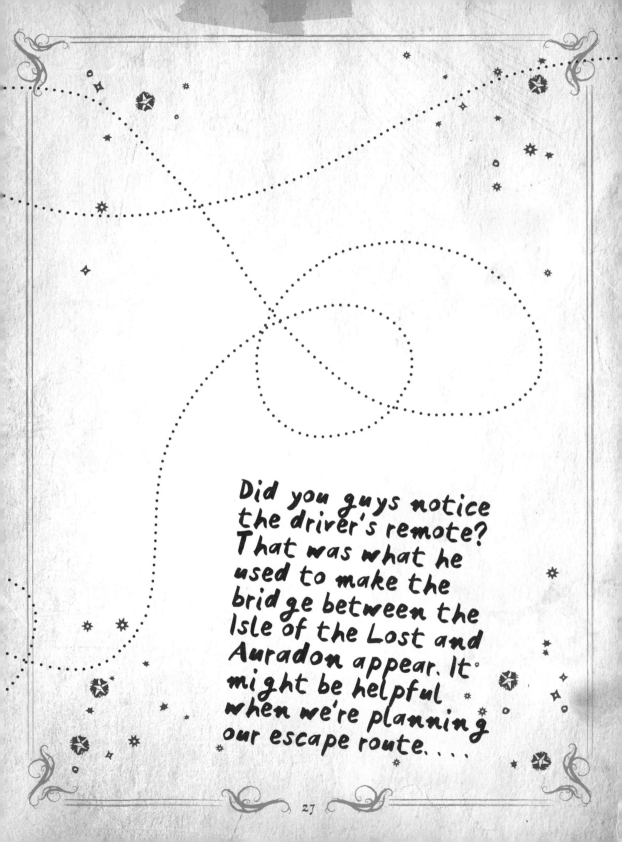

Did you guys notice the driver's remote? That was what he used to make the bridge between the Isle of the Lost and Auradon appear. It might be helpful when we're planning our escape route. . . .

Badness

GOODNESS DOESN'T

GET ANY BETTER

Badder

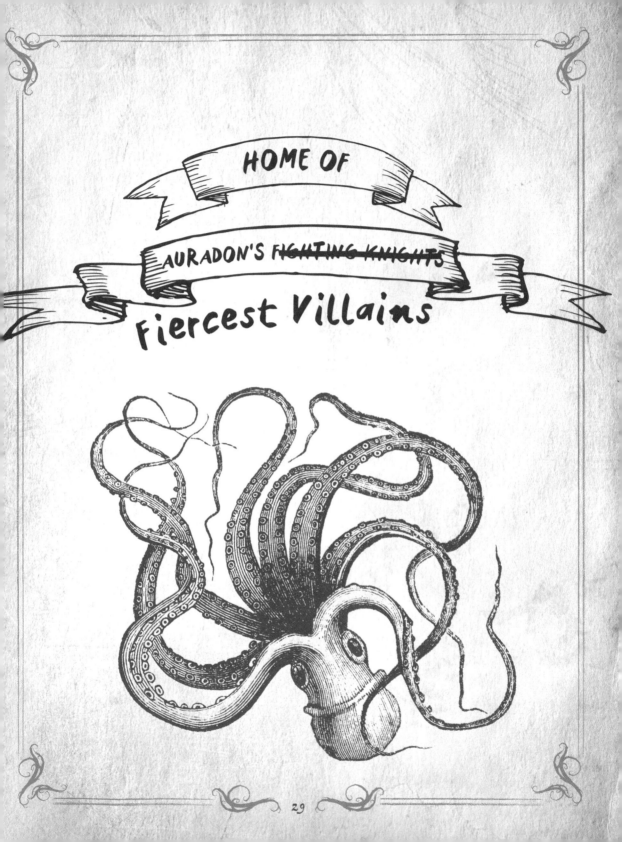

HOME OF

AURADON'S ~~FIGHTING KNIGHTS~~

Fiercest Villains

Carlos! Jay! Talk about making a first impression. Did you really have to stumble out of the limo FIGHTING with each other over that stupid blanket? In front of a whole group of Auradon Prep students? Seriously, we're already outcasts here because of our parents. We don't need to give these kids any more reasons to hate us.

IT WAS JAY'S FAULT! HE ALREADY TOOK THE TELEVISION SET, THE STEREO SYSTEM, THE HOOD ORNAMENT, AND A HANDFUL OF CANDY FROM THE LIMO. WHAT DID HE NEED WITH THAT BLANKET? IT WAS THE ONE THING I WANTED. CAN'T I HAVE A LITTLE SECURITY HERE?

WHATEVER.
I PUT THE STUFF BACK, **JUST** LIKE FAIRY GODMOTHER SAID I SHOULD. I GAVE CARLOS HIS BLANKIE-WANKIE. NO **PERMANENT** DAMAGE DONE. I JUST WISH IT HADN'T HAPPENED IN FRONT OF **AUDREY**, PRINCE BEN'S GIRLFRIEND. SHE'S REALLY CUTE.

Audrey!??!?
You seriously have a crush on Audrey?!?

BARF.

Triskaidekaphobia

A common issue among villains,

The fear of the number thirteen

Can be debilitating if it goes unchecked.

Consult wizards and warlocks for

The best ways to overcome this problem.

Wedding Superstitions

Are you paying attention, Jay?!?

Brides should carry salt in their pockets.

Brides should not be seen fully dressed in a mirror before the ceremony—

JAY + AUDREY FOREVER

It is wise to keep one shoe or one piece of clothing
off until minutes before the ceremony.

A tear in the veil is seen as a sign
of a happy marriage to come.

To ensure luck, the bride must exit with her
right foot first when she crosses the threshold.

It is a bad omen if the bride's car does
not start on the way to the ceremony.

To overcome bad omens, the groom should
carry a miniature horseshoe in his pocket.

OKAY, SO I DON'T KNOW ABOUT YOU GUYS, BUT I WAS EXPECTING THIS BEN KID TO BE A TOTAL NIGHTMARE. LIKE, THE SON OF BELLE AND THE BEAST? HOW COULD HE POSSIBLY BE COOL? BUT I DON'T KNOW. HE'S NOT HALF AS BAD AS I'D THOUGHT HE'D BE. DID YOU GUYS LIKE HIS JOKE ABOUT HIS DAD SHEDDING ON THE COUCH? IT WAS KIND OF FUNNY. . . .

AUDREY IS ANOTHER STORY. SORRY, JAY, YOU'RE ALONE ON THIS ONE.

Audrey   BEN

Did you even hear what Audrey said to me, Jay?!?
THE EVIL QUEEN HAS <u>NO ROYAL STATUS HERE</u>, AND NEITHER
DO YOU. She basically told me I wasn't a princess in
front of all those Auradon Prep kids. I mean, it was
humiliating. We haven't even been here twenty-four
hours and already we're making enemies . . . and for
once, I didn't even do anything to deserve it. I mean,
usually when I make enemies it's on purpose, you know?
Ben does seem cool, Mal. I'll give you that. And he has
that prince hair I like.

Prince hair?!?

Yeah, you know . . . it's all parted on the
side and combed over and moves in the
breeze a little bit. Sigh. ❀

Useful Gemstones

Gemstones can be used
To draw power to an individual,

To protect,

To ward off enemies.

If found or gifted to you,

keep these gemstones.

Their very presence in your home

May strengthen your resolve.

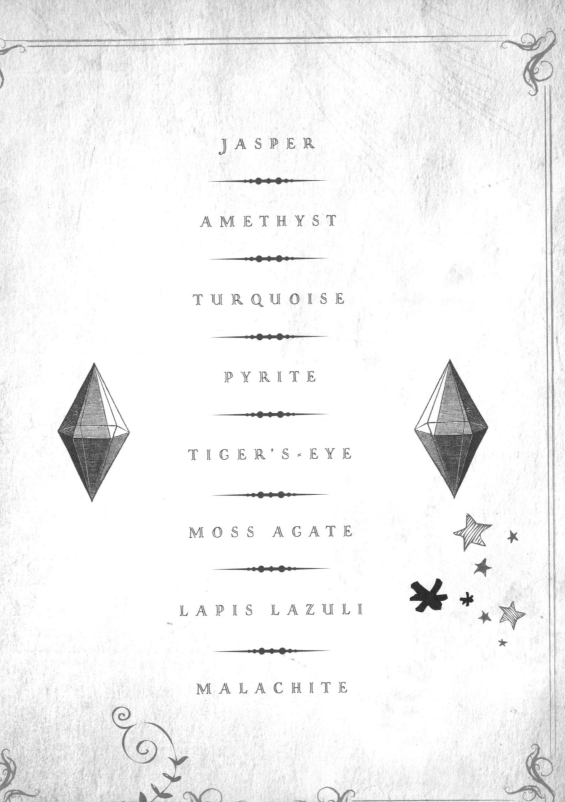

JASPER

AMETHYST

TURQUOISE

PYRITE

TIGER'S-EYE

MOSS AGATE

LAPIS LAZULI

MALACHITE

The WICKED WITCH of Auradon

AT LEAST SHE'S CUTE. ISN'T SHE AURORA'S DAUGHTER?

Basic Princess. Snoozerville.

WIMPY'S KID

HIS NAME IS DOUG, AND HE'S DOPEY'S KID. AND I KIND OF LIKE HIM. HE AND BEN WERE ACTUALLY NICE TO US.

GORGEOUS.

Ugh. A crush already?
We haven't even been
here twenty-four
hours.

HIS NAME'S CHAD, HE'S
CINDERELLA'S SON, AND HE WAS
GIVING ME WEIRD LOOKS.

THEY'RE ALL
GIVING US
WEIRD LOOKS.

OWNER OF
THE WAND

AKA Fairy Godmother

AS LONG AS WE'RE SHARING PHOTOS, LOOK AT THIS OLD PHOTO STRIP I FOUND MIXED IN WITH MY STUFF.

MAL LOOKING SNEAKY

ANNOYED MAL

Whatever, JAY...

SERIOUS MAL

POPPIN' HER COLLAR MAL

Prince Ben, our (hero!) (NOT.)
Son of Belle and the Beast

Is the Beast a big dog?
He kind of looks like one. . . .

I think he's like . . .
a beast? I don't know.

Dear Children of the Isle of the Lost,

Today marks your first day as students of Auradon Prep, the most prestigious academy on Auradon (I'm supposed to mention that—Fairy Godmother asked me to). But perhaps more importantly, it's your first day living somewhere other than the Isle of the Lost. You are no longer under the influence of your parents. Your future is at last yours to decide.

I hope this day goes down in history as the day our peoples began to heal. The day that we, as the future generation, decided what we wanted for ourselves. We don't have to follow the rules from before. Together we can make our own rules, and hopefully we can have a little fun, too.

Does that sound really formal? Maybe . . . Kind of. But I had to write something to make this official. The truth? I really only want to say one thing:

I'm happy you're here.

—Ben

He's dreamy.

WHAT A SUCKER! HE'S NOT GOING TO BE TALKING LIKE THIS WHEN WE'RE RUNNING FROM AURADON WITH THE FAIRY GODMOTHER'S WAND.

He already got one thing wrong; villains NEVER follow the rules.

Incantations

The first chart deals with the
Lunar and solar elements.
The second chart eschews the mastery
Of the solar element or the red stone.

One more thing about Ben: wasn't it funny how he was talking to us in that announcement voice, like he was addressing the entire kingdom or something? He was all: THIS DAY WILL GO DOWN IN HISTORY AS THE DAY OUR PEOPLES BEGAN TO HEAL. It's like he really believes it, that us coming into Auradon is going to change everything. That we're not like our parents, that the choices we'll make will be different. He's so optimistic... I kind of feel sorry for him.

ENOUGH ABOUT BEN! DID YOU SEE THAT STATUE
OF HIS DAD? SERIOUSLY, THE BEAST IS LIKE THE
BIGGEST, SCARIEST DOG I'VE EVER SEEN, WITH HUGE
FANGS AND THICK FUR AND CLAWS TWO INCHES
LONG. HE'S EVERYTHING MY MOM TOLD ME DOGS
WERE—VICIOUS, ANGRY, AND MEAN. NOTE TO SELF:
NEVER MAKE THE KING ANGRY.

The solar element will nest, finally,

In the embalmed corpse, the symbol

Of change, of the perpetual

Revolution of the cycles, the rejoicing

Or springing or sublimation of

The soul.

Those among your throng who desire

To have the most true knowledge,

Of the magickal arts,

Let them peruse these words and chants

And recite them oftentimes over.

BUT IT WAS
COOL HOW BEN
JUST CLAPPED
HIS HANDS AND
CHANGED THE
STATUE INTO
HIS DAD IN
HUMAN FORM.
I DON'T
KNOW WHAT
YOUR MOM WAS
TALKING
ABOUT, MAL.
THERE IS STILL
SOME MAGIC
IN AURADON.

THE MASTERY OVER SELF IS THE MOST
VALUABLE MEASURE IN THE ENTIRE WORLD.

SO I KNOW WE HAVE TO BE HERE—WE'RE GOING TO STEAL THE WAND AND ALL THAT GOOD STUFF—BUT DO WE REALLY HAVE TO GO TO SCHOOL WHILE WE'RE AT IT? LIKE WE ACTUALLY HAVE TO SHOW UP TO CLASS? I THINK I WENT TO SCHOOL THREE TIMES, IF THAT, MY WHOLE LAST YEAR ON THE ISLE OF THE LOST. HOW AM I EVEN GOING TO KEEP UP WITH THIS SCHEDULE? LOOK AT IT.

DRAGON ANATOMY

SAFETY RULES FOR THE INTERNET

GRAMMAR

HISTORY OF AURADON

BASIC CHIVALRY

HISTORY OF WOODSMEN AND PIRATES

MATHEMATICS

REMEDIAL GOODNESS 101

BASIC CHIVALRY. I SIT THROUGH A WEEK OF THAT CLASS AND I'M GOING TO BE LIKE: THANK YOU, MA'AM. YES, PLEASE, I'D LOVE SOME TEA WITH HONEY.

CAN'T WAIT TO SEE THAT!
LOOK ON THE BRIGHT SIDE: AT LEAST YOU
DON'T HAVE TO TAKE HEROISM. HOW AM
I SUPPOSED TO BE A HERO WHEN I CAN'T
EVEN LOOK A PUPPY IN THE EYES?!

There is no bright
side, Carlos!!

Woohoo! It looks like we're
in the same classes except for
DRAGON ANATOMY
AND
BASIC CHIVALRY.

I KNOW YOU'RE NERVOUS ABOUT BASIC CHIVALRY, JAY, BUT SERIOUSLY: REMEDIAL GOODNESS 101? WHAT IS THAT EVEN ABOUT? IT'S INSULTING, LIKE WE CAN'T UNDERSTAND THE MOST OBVIOUS THINGS ABOUT BEING GOOD. I KNOW WHAT'S WRONG AND WHAT'S RIGHT.... I CHOOSE TO BE EVIL.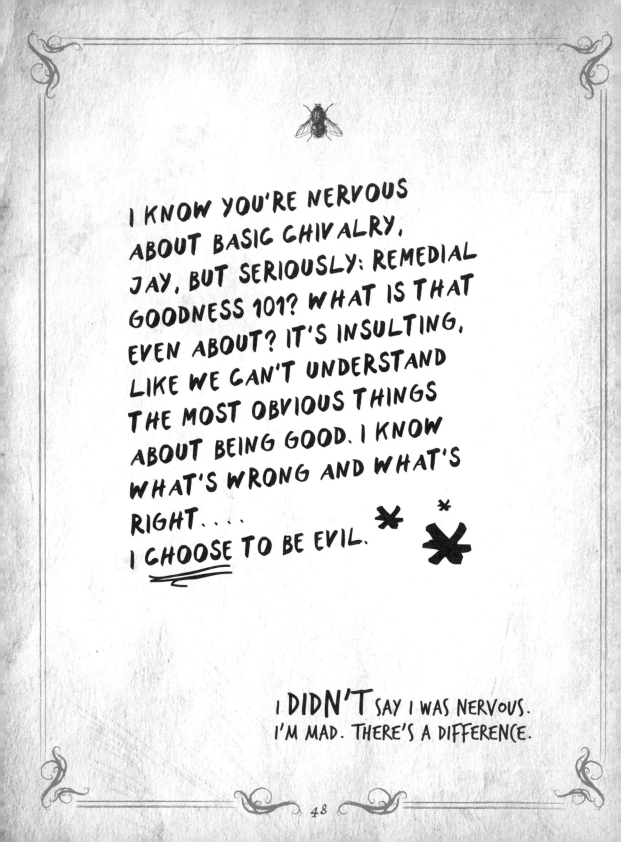

I DIDN'T SAY I WAS NERVOUS. I'M MAD. THERE'S A DIFFERENCE.

Friendship Spell

A bond of friendship is born

The moment you look into my eyes.

Time turns on its head

And I'm given the power to make a foe a friend,

The exhilarating Spirit of the ages

Rising around me.

This might come in handy if we have problems with Audrey. . . .

Invisibility Spell

FIRST

With the' fragments from
A broken amethyst,
Mix sand from a beach
Walked by giants.

SECOND

Grind the' two elements
With a mortar and pestle,
Bringing to a fine' dust.

THIRD

Cast the' dust
In front of you,
Sending it toward the' rafters.

FOURTH

Step into the cloud and
Repeat the following spell
As you're enveloped in powder:

FIFTH

Make me one with the shadows,
Invisible to the eye.
Grant me the gift of moving unseen
Through the world of the living.

Are You "In" or "Invisible"?

When you walk into a room, other students:

A) Come over and say hi.

B) Ignore you

C) Look you up and down, studying your outfit like it's a trash bag.

Everyone thinks it's cool to be on the tourney team at school. You:

A) Are the first one to sign up.

B) Think it's more fun to watch than play.

C) Would rather play video games in your room.

You're going to your first party at school. You:

A) Can't wait. Woohoo!

B) Are a little nervous but excited to see everyone. You hope your outfit is okay. . . .

C) Think, Do I have to go?

During the school dance, where would you be?

A) In the middle of the dance floor showing everyone your sick moves.

B) Hanging by the snacks with your close friends.

C) Hiding out behind the building, wondering why you're there at all.

Your ideal best friend is:

A) A popular kid in school.

B) Your lab partner from chem class—he's a really nice guy.

C) Someone you've known since you were a kid. It's hard for you to trust people.

→ **Mostly A's:** You love hanging out with the in crowd, and they love you.

→ **Mostly B's:** You like meeting new people, but you don't stress about fitting in.

→ **Mostly C's:** You're shy and people don't always notice you, but not everyone wants to be popular.

Thank you, Evie, for helping me shut the curtains. I can't stand this place. It's so not me. Everyone is walking down the halls with these perfect, plastic smiles on their faces. Their shirts are tucked in and their pants and skirts are pleated. It's like they're all about to vomit rainbows, to go on about all the happiness and cheer in the world.

NOT COOL.

WAIT, MAL . . . I'M NOT SURE I GET WHAT YOU'RE SAYING. DO YOU MEAN YOU DON'T LIKE IT HERE???

Whoa. Our room is definitely
fit for two princesses.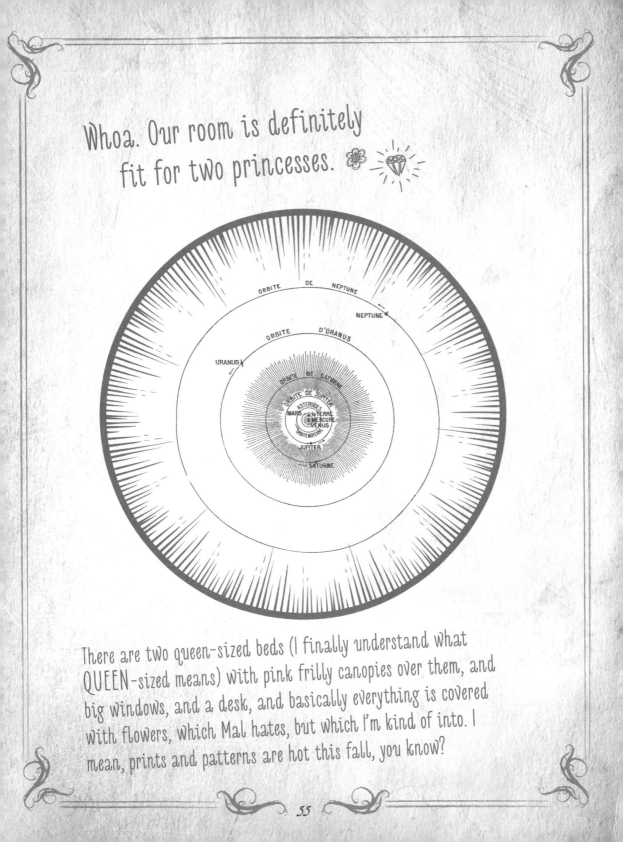

There are two queen-sized beds (I finally understand what
QUEEN-sized means) with pink frilly canopies over them, and
big windows, and a desk, and basically everything is covered
with flowers, which Mal hates, but which I'm kind of into. I
mean, prints and patterns are hot this fall, you know?

Let's look at the pros.

* There are cute princes in Auradon. (You can't deny this, Mal, you really can't. Did you see Chad?!)

* We can go to class here without there being a fight every ten minutes.

* Even if our rooms are too bright and cheery, at least they're clean, and we'll have breakfast waiting for us every morning in the cafeteria. That's more than we can say about home.

Out! Away!

Away from the Blessed Light,
Drift into that psychic night.
The infinite dimensions await thee.

All the while I will do my work,
Until such a time as I will
Return you to day.

**You totally love it here. I don't
even know you anymore.**

I don't, I don't! I'm just saying it's not all bad . . . okay?
Just think of this as a little vacation in a fancy Auradon
hotel. That's what I'm trying to do. . . .

How to Detect Deception

A liar's words are deceptive by nature,
But to be deceived you must first believe.

To prevent deception, study the speaker's
Expression— the corners of his mouth,
Whether the nostrils are flared, where his gaze lies.
Then incant beneath the breath:

WORDS OF WONDER AND QUESTION,

DO YOU DECEIVE THE ONE
YOU SPEAK TO?

CAN THE EAR WHICH HEARS
TRUST YOUR WORDS?

IS THERE AN ERRANT
WILL IN YOUR HEART?

I'M WITH EVIE, MAL. YOU CAN'T JUST KEEP SAYING THIS IS THE WORST PLACE IN THE WORLD—NOT WHEN THERE ARE SOME DEFINITE UPSIDES. LIKE CARLOS'S AND MY ROOM? IT'S TOTALLY SOUPED UP. FLAT-SCREEN TVS ON THE WALLS. SURROUND-SOUND SPEAKERS. A VIDEO GAME CONSOLE.

If the Speaker Speaks of false notions,
The whites of the eyes will turn pink,
The nostrils will flare,
The corners of the mouth will turn up,
A dragon's expression, if only for a moment.
You will see.

PLUS, ALL THESE AURADON PREP KIDS ARE RICH! I'VE ALREADY STOLEN FIVE CELL PHONES, TWO IPADS, AND THREE WALLETS. THAT IS SOME SERIOUS LOOT.

OKAY. JOURNEY INTO THE ENCHANTED FOREST?!?! WHO ELSE HAS PLAYED THIS BESIDES ME AND JAY?!? DO YOU GUYS EVEN HAVE A VIDEO GAME SYSTEM IN YOUR ROOM??? SERIOUSLY, THOUGH, THIS GAME IS AWESOME. YOU'RE A WIZARD MOVING THROUGH THE ENCHANTED FOREST, AND EVIL FAIRIES COME AFTER YOU, TRYING TO CAST SPELLS ON YOU AS REVENGE FOR SOME PARTY YOU DIDN'T INVITE THEM TO. I'M UP TO LEVEL TEN ALREADY AND I'VE ONLY BEEN PLAYING FOR TWO HOURS. I'M GOING TO TRY TO BEAT THE GAME BEFORE WE LEAVE—I HAVE TO.

Are you two kidding me?!? Jay: How can you be concerned about stealing when we're about to take over all of Auradon, then the entire world?!? You get busted for taking some kid's wallet, they're going to be on to us. We don't need all the teachers at Auradon Prep watching us every minute of every day.

AND, CARLOS: I can't believe you like that game. Evil fairies that chase you through the forest trying to cast spells on you? Do you even know who they're referring to? Journey into the Enchanted Forest is definitely a slam on my mom, for sure. Find out who made the game . . . I'll add them to my list of People Deserving of Revenge.

Okay. I played Journey into the Enchanted Forest today with Carlos, and I'm sorry, Mal, I really am, but I have to agree . . . it's incredible. We were trapped behind this waterfall for what seemed like an hour, and then these evil fairies attacked us and we had to get them off by throwing water on their wings so they couldn't fly. They were all lying on the ground and we finally got away and ran down the mountain, then found a bush of elderberries to eat to regain our strength.

You have to play, Mal— loyalties aside, you would love it.

I do not have to play. And I will not love it. Get your head in the game, guys! (The real game, not the video game.) We have a magic wand to steal!

WE KILLED IT TODAY, EVIE! WOOHOO! LEVEL **TWELVE** COMING OUR WAY!!

You don't have to worry, Mal. I have my head in the game (the real game, not the video game). I found the Fairy Godmother's magic wand in my mother's mirror tonight, did I not? It says it's at the Museum of Cultural History, whatever that is.
→ → → WE'RE GETTING CLOSER. . . ← ← ←
Magic Mirror, in my hand, who's the fairest in the land?

WHAT TO WATCH OUT FOR IN AURADON

HEROES WITH GOOD INTENTIONS (GOOD INTENTIONS ARE THE WORST.)

ANYONE WHO CRITICIZES THE ISLE OF THE LOST

ANYONE WHO CRITICIZES OUR PARENTS

ANYONE WHO ASKS TOO MANY QUESTIONS (IF WE'RE GOING TO CARRY OUT OUR PLAN, WE NEED TO MAKE SURE NO ONE IS SUSPICIOUS OF US.)

ANYONE WHO WANTS TO CHANGE US (THEY DON'T GET THAT WE LIKE BEING VILLAINS.)

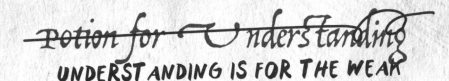

~~Potion for Understanding~~

UNDERSTANDING IS FOR THE WEAK

You sound just like
your mom, Mal.

To understand thine' enemy
Is a power unparalleled.
knowing what a foe' wants, needs,
And values is strength.

I take that as
a compliment.
Thank you.

Create' this elixir
And drink it, just three' drops,
To gain insight into another's mind:

2 DROPS OLEANDER EXTRACT

1 DROP LEMONGRASS

1 DROP VINEGAR

1 TEASPOON GROUND RAT SPLEEN

1 TEASPOON HORSEHAIR

EWWWWWW, GROSS!

No Rest for the Wicked

At times, it may be imperative
To remain conscious
For several days at once,
Especially if one
Is in the midst of plotting
Or about to carry out an evil plan.

Recite this spell three times
While on a line of power.
You will only be able to sleep
When you reverse the spell
with the words

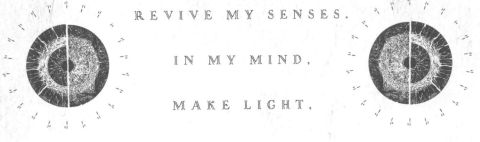

TO SLEEP,

A SWEET RELEASE, ONE I ASK FOR NOW.

AWAKE! ALIVE!

REVIVE MY SENSES.

IN MY MIND,

MAKE LIGHT,

THE PERCEPTION OF A CONTINUOUS DAY.

KEEP ME UP ALL HOURS

UNTIL I SAY THE WORDS OF REVERSAL.

Evie's Fashion Tips for Prep School

Uniforms don't have to be dull and drab. Follow these tips to take your skirt and polo from frump to fashionista.

* Play with hemlines. Rips, tears, and jagged edges are hot right now.
* Accessorize, accessorize, accessorize. Try colorful hair clips, chunky jeweled necklaces, and patterned tights.
* As my mother always says, you can never wear enough makeup. Dramatic eyeliner will draw attention to your dark, angular features.
* A dark nail polish can create a more sophisticated, edgier look.
* Nothing says "rebellion" like a black combat boot.

Tonight we go to the Museum of Cultural History. Finally, Jay, you'll be able to put all your thievery to good use. Remember: we have to stick together. Evie, you walk at the back of the group and keep watch to make sure no one follows us off the campus. We have to break curfew on this one, and we can't get caught....

So, according to a quick search on my laptop, this place—the Museum of Cultural History—houses all these artifacts from Auradon's history, both good and evil. That's why Fairy Godmother's magic wand is there. There are statues of our parents in the Gallery of Villains and even the spindle Audrey's mom pricked her finger on. It's only two miles away. We should head out as soon as it gets dark

A Villain's Lair

A lair must be <u>dark and dank</u>,
Filled with Spiders,
<u>Covered in dust</u>.
Thick curtains to <u>block out the</u> sun
Must hang from every window.

Do <u>not</u> allow the light of day in.
Do <u>not</u> permit enthusiasm or cheer.
No <u>happy thoughts</u> should be thought,
<u>Not here</u>.

*See?? This is what I'm
talking about! No lace or
pom-pom pillowcases!*

EVIL LURKS WHERE GOODNESS

CANNOT FIND IT.

STAY HIDDEN.

STAY PROTECTED.

Fairy Blessings

To be blessed by a fairy

Is one of the most precious gifts.

If possible, save the dust cast from her wings.

It will prove invaluable for conjuring.

What happens in the Museum of Cultural History stays in the Museum of Cultural History. Except when you're keeping a record of your time on Auradon with three of your best friends and you need to record every detail of the greatest takeover ever. This will definitely be one for the history books. So, Carlos, I know you think Mal's spell book is lame, but you have to admit, when we got to the museum and saw that guard at the entrance, there was no easy way to get around him. Then she whipped out this spell book, and voilà: the guard was asleep within seconds.

Carlos: maybe we can use this in
Journey into the Enchanted Forest.

I do hereby declare this, the Hypnotic Sleep Spell, to be the very first spell my good friend Mal used in Auradon. It was used one crisp night on the guard at the Museum of Cultural History. As soon as she spoke the words from this spell, the guard's eyes glassed over. Then he stood up and walked right over to Aurora's spindle and pricked his finger on it, falling fast asleep. Um, that's a successful spell if I ever saw one.

YEAH, BUT DO WE NEED TO USE SPELLS ON EVERYTHING?  AFTER THE GUARD WENT DOWN, I WANTED TO KICK DOWN THE DOOR INTO THE MUSEUM, BUT MAL INSISTED SHE USE MAGIC TO OPEN IT. THIS SPELL BOOK IS RUINING ALL MY FUN.

Do not even start with me, Jay. You nearly cost us everything last night. As soon as you saw the wand, you just lunged for it. You didn't even think about force fields or alarms or anything. Were you <u>trying</u> to get us caught?

ME?!?! YOU SHOULD HAVE JUST LET ME GO TO THE MUSEUM ALONE, LIKE I WANTED TO. I SAID I COULD GET IT BY MYSELF. I'M BETTER AT STEALING WHEN I DO IT ON MY OWN TERMS. BESIDES, IF YOU HADN'T ZONED OUT IN THE GALLERY OF VILLAINS, STARING UP AT THAT STATUE OF YOUR MOM, MAYBE WE WOULD'VE HAD MORE TIME TO FIGURE OUT HOW TO GET THE MAGIC WAND.

Hypnotic Sleep Spell

Hear my entreaty ㅈㅈㅈ

To the old ones I owe my loyalty.

Magic Spindle, do not linger.

Make my victim prick a finger.

Torque of hypnosis,

Build a cone of power.

Import the urge for natural sleep,

Whatever may be the hour.

When after a time, he may wake,

Naught of these workings

May his senses take.

The hour is here to let thine body

repose and gently drift away.

MAGIC MIRRORS

A magic mirror is an asset
To any witch,
Giving them the power to gaze into
The future,
To see scenes beyond their view,
And to locate objects that have gone missing.

The most common magic mirrors
Do not speak to the viewer,
But instead reveal truth in images.

Magic mirrors can also be used to reverse hexes.

They can also be used to apply lipstick
or tweeze your eyebrows. ☺

Mal . . . I hate to admit it, but Jay does have a point. We were all kind of feeling freaked out and rushed, and when he saw the wand . . . well, he just lunged at it. How was he supposed to know there'd be a force field and an alarm? And that it would wake up the guard from the Hypnotic Sleep Spell?

COME ON, WHAT DOES IT MATTER NOW, GUYS? IT'S NOT WORTH FIGHTING ABOUT, OR ARGUING ABOUT WHO DID WHAT OR WHO SHOULD HAVE DONE THIS OR THAT. WHO CARES? WE'RE BACK AT AURADON PREP, AND WE DIDN'T GET CAUGHT, THANKS TO YOURS TRULY. CAN'T WE JUST BE THANKFUL FOR THAT?

That's right! We all owe Carlos a thank-you for thinking fast and answering the phone. If he hadn't pretended to be the guard and said everything was okay, they might've sent the Auradon police to the museum. Then everyone would've found out we were there. We'd probably be on a bus back to the Isle of the Lost right now. There's no way we can go back to the museum—it's not worth the risk—so we'll have to figure out a way to bring the magic wand to us. Let's just keep working together, okay?

FINE.
THANK YOU, CARLOS.
BUT SERIOUSLY: A FORCE FIELD AND AN ALARM? THAT'S JUST EXCESSIVE.

Thanks, C.
I'm going to stop arguing about this, like you said, C. We'll figure out another way to get the wand. Now i'll leave you three with a quote from my dear mother, maleficent:

"DON'T YOU WANT TO BE HEARTLESS AND HARDENED AS STONE?

DON'T YOU WANT TO BE FINGER-LICKIN EVIL TO THE BONE?"

WHY WOULD WE WANT TO?

Because we might be here a while . . . duh.

❧ HOW TO GET THE MOST OUT OF AURADON PREP ❧

1) Take in the sights! Enchanted lakes, fields of green, rainbow skies. There are so many cute princes, too! Keep your eyes open as you walk around the quad, and be sure to enjoy the scenery, if you know what I mean.

2) Royal balls or social functions are a good chance to network. Be enchanting and sweet. Pretending to be good is great practice for other manipulations.

> Be wise to honor the return
> Of the love object into your
> Sphere of influence.
> Await the beloved with a quiet certainty,
> Like the knowledge— the certainty—
> Of the coming dawn, the turning of
> The day into the gloaming.

3) Having breakfast, lunch, and dinner prepared for you every day is a special treat. Take advantage of the Auradon Prep dining hall (especially on ice cream sundae days—yum).

4) Quiet hours in the dorm are a good time to sew, draw, journal, or do anything else you don't have time to do on the Isle of the Lost.

LOVE WITH THE WHOLE OF YOUR BEING

So as to harness the natural
Magick that resides in the very
Core of your being, your heart,
your soul.

LET THE PROCESS BE THE GOAL.

On guardians of love and fortune,
May my will create tangible

Okay, okay. I'm not going to keep harping on this, but there is another MAJOR benefit of getting the wand sooner rather than later. Today was the first day of class, and I don't know about you guys, but I can't stay here another two or three weeks. Remedial Goodness class is killing me.

I DO LIKE THE IDEA OF NOT GOING TO SCHOOL ANYMORE.
CARLOS AND I WERE REALLY SWEATING DURING BASIC CHIVALRY.
I MEAN, HAVE YOU GUYS HEARD ABOUT ALL THESE DIFFERENT
RULES? LIKE, OUR TEACHER MADE US SIT DOWN IN FRONT OF THIS
PLATE THAT HAD TWO FORKS, A KNIFE, AND TWO SPOONS.
I HAD NO IDEA WHAT WAS USED FOR WHAT.

EFFECT. FOLLOW THE WAY OF VIRTUE

In the full visage of the father
And the mother, the sun and the moon,
And all of the twelve houses.

HEAR ME.

May my will be done.

BASIC CHIVALRY WAS NOTHING COMPARED TO
HEROISM. THEY HAD ME SWINGING FROM THIS
ROPE INTO A PIT OF FOAM BLOCKS, THEN RUNNING
AS FAST AS I COULD TO THE OTHER SIDE OF THE
GYM. I WAS HYPERVENTILATING FOR TEN MINUTES.
SERIOUSLY, WHY DO THEY THINK I COULD BE A
HERO?!? I JUST WANT TO GO BACK TO THE ISLE OF
THE LOST, WHERE NO ONE EXPECTS MUCH OF ME.

I've been in class one day and I think I'm already failing Chemistry. Is that possible?

Oh, and here's a little Remedial Goodness quiz for my favorite Auradon Prep students:

YOU PASS A STRANGER WHO'S FALLEN AND TWISTED HIS ANKLE. HE'S BEGGING FOR YOUR HELP. DO YOU:

a) Keep walking.

b) Grab his wallet because you know he can't chase you.

c) Pretend you don't hear him.

d) Call for help on your cell phone and wait with him until someone arrives.

e) None of the above.

This one's tricky....

B! EASY LOOT!

D. D—D—D—DUH.

MY TURN! POP QUIZ:

YOU SEE A DOG RUNNING IN THE MIDDLE OF THE STREET. HE HAS A COLLAR AND OBVIOUSLY BELONGS TO SOMEONE, BUT IF YOU DON'T DO ANYTHING, HE MIGHT GET HIT BY A CAR. DO YOU:

A) STOP TRAFFIC AND GRAB HIM. HE'S CUTE; HE'LL MAKE A GREAT NEW PET.

B) PRETEND YOU DON'T SEE HIM. KEEP WALKING.

C) GRAB HIM AND CALL HIS OWNERS TO SEE HOW MUCH THE REWARD IS. IF IT'S NOTHING, THEN LET HIM GO.

D) PICK HIM UP AND BRING HIM TO THE ADDRESS ON HIS TAG.

E) NONE OF THE ABOVE.

I USUALLY GO WITH THE STEALING OPTION, BUT THIS TIME . . . MAYBE D.

E. NONE OF THE ABOVE. IF I SAW A DOG, I'D RUN AS FAST AS I COULD IN THE OTHER DIRECTION.

We forgot to discuss the best part of Remedial Goodness 101: Jane, the Fairy Godmother's daughter. She's what Ursula the sea witch would call a poor unfortunate soul.

SHE DEFINITELY THOUGHT WE WERE GOING TO BITE HER HEAD OFF OR SOMETHING. I'VE NEVER SEEN ANYONE SO AFRAID OF ME IN MY ENTIRE LIFE.

Never? You don't give yourself enough credit, Jay. . . .

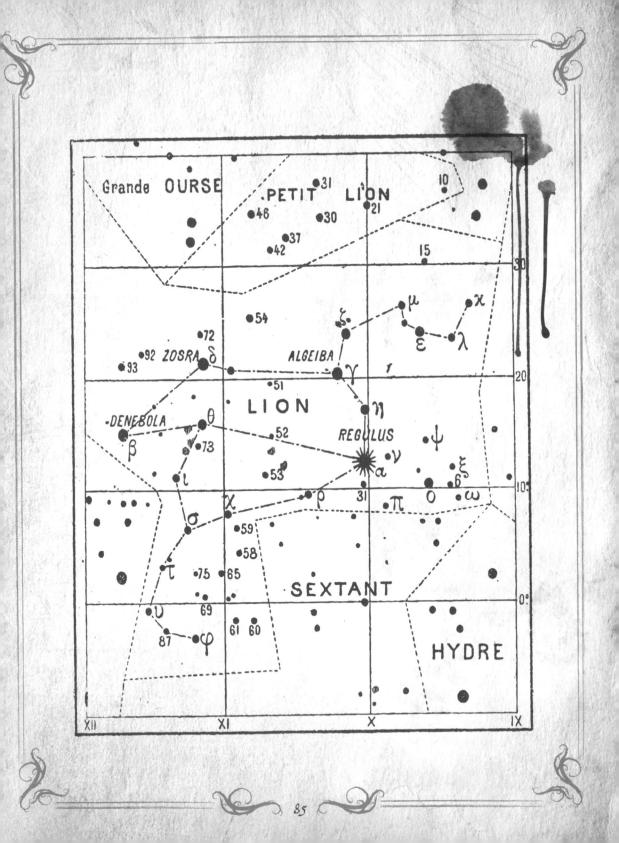

Chant to the Master

THRILL WITH THE WARMTH OF THE

Morning sun.
Out of the crepuscular
Glow it comes.

FROM THE GUARDIANS OF THE EAST

And the West, riding leviathans
O'er the seas.

YOU HAVE ARRIVED, MY MASTER, MY

Teacher, my light.

LIKE THE MOON IN THE WOODS,

Emitting its argentine glow; like
The dimpled dawn of autumnal

Repose.

STEP ONTO DRY LAND, MY MASTER,

My teacher,
My light.

LIGHT YOUR BLACK ALTAR CANDLES AND

Hold your athame high and walk deosil
Exclaim with this blade, I cast
The circle of my craft.

EXISTENCE IS A WONDROUS, COMPLEX

Tapestry of laws and concomitant
Movements of matter and cosmic energies.

THIS MAGICAL ARMATURE REVEALS THE

Living structures of the existential
Plane; it provides an instruction on
How magic fits into nature, and how
Nature functions, from the dense
Levels to the rarefied realms.

THROUGH THIS ARCANE KNOWLEDGE, A

Person comes to know where they are
In relation to the universe.

I've been thinking more about Jane, Fairy Godmother's daughter. Yes, she has bad hair, and yes, she's in desperate need of a makeover, but she might just be the key to getting the magic wand out of the Museum of Cultural History....

❋ ❋ * ❋ * ❋ ❋ * ❋ *

What do you mean? You think they'll give her access to it?

I have to do some digging. Stay tuned....

EVIE, MAL: YOU'RE SO LUCKY YOU'RE NOT GUYS. SERIOUSLY. HEROISM CLASS WAS NOTHING COMPARED TO TOURNEY PRACTICE. YOU WOULDN'T BELIEVE THIS GAME. SO THERE ARE ACTUAL CANNONS AT EITHER END OF THE FIELD (THEY'RE CALLED THE REAPERS) AND THEY SHOOT BALLS AT US WHILE WE'RE RUNNING, TRYING TO GET TO THE OTHER SIDE. THE FIELD IS CALLED THE KILL ZONE, AND IT'S NO JOKE. SERIOUSLY, I ALMOST DIED THERE.

COME ON, CARLOS, THE ACTUAL GAME WASN'T THAT BAD. THE OTHER KIDS? NOW THAT WAS THE PROBLEM. EVIE, I KNOW YOU'VE BEEN GOING ON ABOUT THAT KID CHAD, CINDERELLA'S SON, BUT I NEARLY GOT IN A FIGHT WITH HIM TODAY. HE THINKS HE'S SO COOL. HE SAID SOMETHING NASTY ABOUT MY DAD AND HOW HE TALKS TO PARROTS. I MEAN,

WHO DOES THIS KID THINK HE IS?

OKAY, MORE INFO: JAY DOESN'T THINK THE GAME IS THAT BAD BECAUSE HE'S ONLY BEEN HERE TWO DAYS AND HE'S ALREADY THE STAR OF THE TEAM. HE CAN OUTRUN ALMOST ANYONE. WHEN HE HAS THE BALL, NO ONE IS ABLE TO GET HIM. I GUESS ALL THOSE DAYS JUMPING FROM ROOF TO ROOF, TRYING NOT TO CAUGHT STEALING, REALLY PAID OFF.

I WASN'T EXAGGERATING BEFORE.
I TOTALLY GOT CREAMED.
IF IT WASN'T FOR BEN, I PROBABLY WOULD HAVE BRAIN DAMAGE, REALLY.

What do you mean "if it wasn't for Ben"? What, did he block a pass or something?

No. I WAS LYING ON THE GROUND WITH MY HANDS OVER MY HEAD AND ALL THE TOURNEY PLAYERS WERE RUNNING RIGHT AT ME. THEY WOULD'VE **TRAMPLED ME.** BEN CAME OVER AND HELPED ME UP, THEN TOLD THE COACH HE SHOULDN'T CUT ME. HE TOLD HIM HE'D HELP ME PRACTICE AND HE WAS SURE I'D BE A QUICK LEARNER.

What is the deal with this Ben guy?!?
WHY IS HE SO NICE?!?
It's totally suspect.

SORRY, CARLOS.
HONESTLY, I DIDN'T SEE YOU THERE. OTHERWISE I WOULD'VE HELPED YOU UP MYSELF.

YEAH, YOU WERE TOO BUSY WAVING TO ALL THOSE GIRLS IN THE STANDS. THAT'S THE OTHER BIG PIECE OF NEWS FROM TOURNEY PRACTICE: JAY IS THE NEW AURADON PREP HEARTTHROB. ALL THE LADIES LOVE HIM.

The Phases of the Moon

When casting Spells, it's
Important to understand the phases
of
The moon, as some Spells will
Undoubtedly call for a Specific
Time in the lunar cycle.

TIPS FOR DEALING WITH A GOODY TWO-SHOES

DO use her good intentions against her. She wants to believe you're good, so she'll often give you the benefit of the doubt, even when it's stupid for her to.

DO pretend to be nice, even if you don't want to be. It gives you the advantage of surprise.

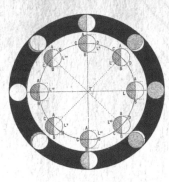

New moon

Waxing crescent

First quarter

Waxing gibbous

Full moon

Waning gibbous

Third quarter

Waning crescent

DO try to influence her friends. If they like you, it'll be harder for her to strike back against you.

DON'T let her make you the butt of jokes. Be ready with a quick, witty reply.

DON'T let her insult you or your family. When attacked, firmly correct her.

DON'T see her outside of school. Limiting your interactions will help you keep your distance.

WHAT TO DO WHEN YOU MEET A CUTE GIRL

→ ON THE ISLE OF THE LOST: SAY, "HEY, WANT TO GO PICK SOME POCKETS?"

→ IN AURADON: SAY, "I'D LOVE TO TAKE YOU TO DINNER SOMETIME."

→ ON THE ISLE OF THE LOST: IF SHE'S COMING DOWN THE STREET, LEAN AGAINST THE WALL AND LOOK COOL. IGNORE HER.

→ IN AURADON: STAND UP STRAIGHT WHEN SHE PASSES. LOOK HER DIRECTLY IN THE EYE AND SMILE TO LET HER KNOW YOU'VE NOTICED HER.

→ ON THE ISLE OF THE LOST: IF YOU'RE HANGING OUT, DO SOMETHING GROSS IN FRONT OF HER AND MAKE A JOKE ABOUT HER TO YOUR FRIENDS. SHE'LL THINK YOU DON'T LIKE HER, WHICH WILL MAKE HER CRAZY.

→ IN AURADON: WHEN YOU'RE WITH HER IN A GROUP, GIVE HER YOUR ATTENTION AND TELL HER SHE LOOKS PRETTY. SHE EXPECTS TO BE TREATED LIKE A PRINCESS.

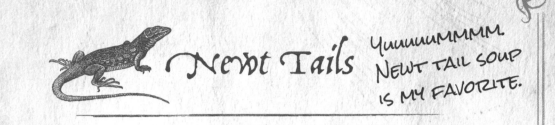

Newt Tails

Newt tails are known

To restore memory loss

Brought on by a curse or by age.

Simmer for an hour

In two tablespoons

Unicorn's blood

IF UNICORN'S BLOOD IS NOT AVAILABLE,

THE BLOOD OF A BLACK STALLION

WILL SUFFICE.

I know you guys are both excited about tourney (or at least you are, Jay), but seriously, all I wanted was to join the cheer squad. I can do a roundoff and three back handsprings. That's more than any other girl on the squad can do. But still, there's no way Audrey will let me on. She controls everything. It's like this one small thing that would actually make life in Auradon bearable . . . I'm not even allowed that.

AUDREY

I'M DEFINITELY NOT EXCITED ABOUT TOURNEY. BUT YEAH, I'M SORRY YOU'RE UPSET, E. THAT'S A TOTAL BUMMER.

Evie, you do a better back handspring than all those girls combined. THAT'S THE TRUTH (and I hate telling the truth). Don't worry about it. I have a plan for getting us out of here sooner rather than later. No more waiting around for Audrey to give us permission to breathe.

DID I MENTION THAT BEN'S GOING TO HELP ME PRACTICE TOURNEY? I DON'T KNOW IF I EVEN WANT TO DO THIS. . . . I MEAN, WHAT'S THE POINT IN PLAYING IF I'M JUST GOING TO GET BANGED UP THE WHOLE TIME? WHY IS IT, LIKE, A REQUIREMENT OR SOMETHING THAT EVERY GUY LIKES SPORTS? CAN'T I JUST LIKE PLAYING VIDEO GAMES WITH EVIE OR HANGING OUT IN MY ROOM?

I WON'T LET YOU GET BANGED UP, CARLOS. PROMISE. JUST START PRACTICING WITH BEN, AND THE NEXT TIME YOU'RE ON THAT TOURNEY FIELD, **I GOT YOUR BACK.** WE'LL TURN THE KILL ZONE INTO THE CARLOS-IS-KILLING-IT ZONE.

THANKS, MAN. ☺

YOU'RE WELCOME!

If you're wondering why I'm writing "you're welcome," it's because you're all going to thank me later. Let me explain.

Today I was standing by my locker when Ben, aka Mr. Nice Guy, came up to me and started going on and on about how I like to draw and I should take art classes at Auradon Prep, and do I like painting blah blah blah blah. I wasn't really paying attention, because I was too distracted by Jane, who slipped into the bathroom across the hall. As soon as I got rid of Ben, I followed her right in. We started chatting, and I noticed how sad and lonely she seems. (I know, I know, it's all kind of obvious.) Then I gave her a new hairdo with a spell. Two minutes later she was staring at her reflection in the mirror, asking if I could help fix her nose. I told her I couldn't.

WAIT . . . WHAT DOES THIS HAVE TO DO WITH US?

Spell For Divine Tresses

May the elemental forces
Infiltrate the root.

Command and sway the course
Of the growth.

Bend toward my will and be as
Fashioned as a homunculus under
The divine architect's hand.

Follicle bulb, feel mine
Etheric energies.

When the circle is complete,
A recitation is moot.

A Spell for a Better Complexion

PIMPLES, PUSS, AND POCKMARKS,

WHITEHEADS AND BLACKHEADS,

SCARS AND MOLES SPROUTING HAIR.

These are the woes of a Witch
Whose genes have been unkind.

Use this Spell to remedy issues
With your complexion.

I shouldn't have to remind you about Cinderella, but I will. Cinderella was a sad, lonely girl with bad hair and bad clothes, until one day Fairy Godmother, aka our Remedial Goodness 101 teacher, decided to give her a little makeover ... using her magic wand. She turned Cinderella from zero to hero in less than ten seconds flat. So. While Jane was staring at her new hair in the mirror, I made a little suggestion: couldn't her mom use her magic wand to give her own daughter a bigger makeover? I mean, if she

Set down a picture or a drawing of
A woman whose complexion you admire.
Using ocean salt, draw a circle around it.
Then recite this spell while gazing
Into the woman's eyes.

Clear away impurities, refine my skin.
Let others see
The light of beauty that is inside. From now forward
I will not be ashamed.

was willing to do it for Cinderella, some girl
she barely knew, why wouldn't she do it for
Jane? And when she did, could I please, pretty
please, be there to watch?

You are a GENIUS, Mal. When is the makeover taking
place? And can I please, pretty please, watch, too?

I'm waiting to hear from Jane.
Let's play it cool for a while and
see what she says, okay?
Remember: no one should mention
anything to anyone about this.
Understand?!?

Got it.

I KNOW WE NEED JANE TO GET
TO HER MOTHER'S WAND, BUT
DOES SHE REALLY THINK SHE
NEEDS A MAKEOVER NOW? LIKE,
SHE WAS SERIOUSLY CRYING
ABOUT HER NOSE?

THAT MAKES ME KIND OF SAD.

Don't go weak on me now, G.
We just have to get the magic wand. Then
we're out of here. Let's try not to overthink it.

You guys . . . you're not going to believe what just happened.

❧ CHAD ASKED ME OUT. ❧

I wasn't paying attention during Chem.
Then Mr. Delay asked me to come to the board and work out the average atomic weight of silver. As I was walking up, I looked down at my mirror and conjured the answer.
Then, while everyone in class was laughing and snickering at me, I copied it all out. CORRECTLY.
Mr. Delay was more than a little surprised.

And I guess Chad was, too. As I was walking back to my desk, he gave me this killer smile and slipped me a note.
It said . . . wait for it . . .

MEET ME UNDER THE
BLEACHERS AT 3.

Erie . . . I don't know about this guy. But I guess if you're happy, I'm happy, right?

Thanks, Mal. I am.
VERY happy. ☺

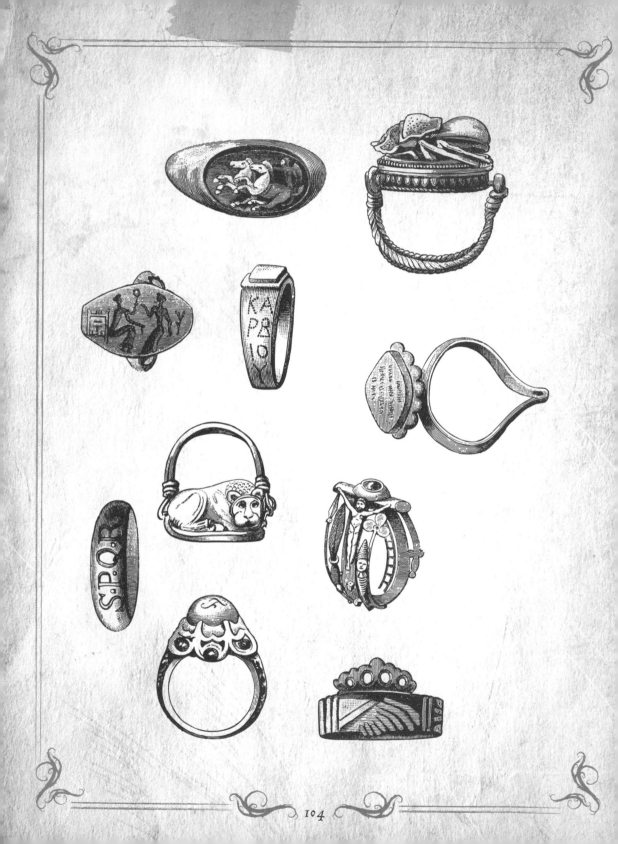

Maybe I should use that for my mom's roots. →
Did I tell you guys about training today? Mal, I
know you're skeptical about Ben, but he seriously
helped me so much. He met me on the track early
this morning. He brought his stopwatch to time
me and even helped me get over my fear of a dog
that started chasing me. Apparently the dog's
name is Dude, and he's the campus mutt. I was
totally freaking out. I told Ben about how my
mom said dogs were bad, and that when they were
wagging their tails, that meant they were about to
attack. But then Dude did the weirdest thing...
he didn't attack. He just licked me and rolled over.
He was actually really sweet.

I HATE TO SAY THIS, CARLOS, BUT I ALWAYS THOUGHT
YOUR MOM WAS A FEW HAIRS SHORT OF A FULL COAT.
YOU KNOW WHAT I'M SAYING?

No...

But seriously, Mal. I really
like Ben. And I really like Dude.
They're both pretty cool.

Okay... I trust you. It
sounds like Ben's at least
still PRETENDING to be nice.

This, for the record, is what I used on Jane! It's better than any shampoo and conditioner combo ever made. It turned her boring hair into flowing waves.

A Spell for Better Hair

Beware, forswear,

Replace the old with new hair.

You're such a skeptic, Mal! I don't have a ton of time to write here, but I wanted to update you on the Chad situation. So we were under the bleachers and he was saying all this sweet stuff, about how I'm really pretty and really smart and everything. I mentioned my magic mirror and how I use it to get all the answers. Then we were talking about Fairy Godmother's wand, and he was staring at me with those huge blue eyes, and then he was leaning in. . . .

We almost kissed.

ALMOST. But then he got panicked and remembered he had tons of homework. So I agreed to help him with some of it. I mean, I feel like that's okay, right? I can do it faster with the mirror. . . .

I. DO.
NOT.
LIKE.
THIS.
GUY.

DRAGON ANATOMY...........................A-
SAFETY RULES FOR THE INTERNET.......B+
GRAMMAR....................................B-
HISTORY OF AURADON....................B-
BASIC CHIVALRY...........................B-
HISTORY OF WOODSMEN AND PIRATES....A
MATHEMATICS..............................B+
REMEDIAL GOODNESS 101.................B

CHECK THIS OUT, GUYS! I ACTUALLY GOT GOOD
GRADES . . . OR DECENT, AT LEAST. HOW
CRAZY IS THAT?!?!

WAY TO GO, MAN!

A Spell to Cure Halitosis

Dragon's breath,
It's commonly called:
A putrid, rotting Stench
Emanating from the mouth.

How do you cure frustration?!?! What about the fear of failure?!?

MIX THE FOLLOWING IN AN OAK BOWL

AND GARGLE THREE TIMES A DAY

UNTIL IT IS CURED.

2 teaspoons vanilla essence

2 lavender Sprigs

1 pinch cat hair

1 pinch ground rhino hide

2 ground gardenia petals

1 cup water from an ogre's well

AGHHHHHHHH.

That is the sound of me tearing out my hair. Better mine than Jane's. Turns out it's off, guys. She wasn't able to convince Fairy Godmother to do a makeover on her. Some nonsense about beauty being on the inside, not the outside.

What world does she live in?!?

Auradon.

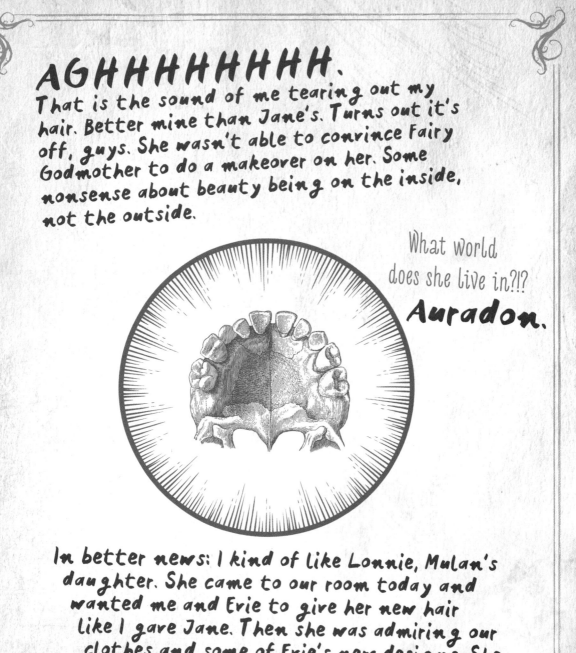

In better news: I kind of like Lonnie, Mulan's daughter. She came to our room today and wanted me and Evie to give her new hair like I gave Jane. Then she was admiring our clothes and some of Evie's new designs. She even said how cool we were. For the first time since we got here, I felt something really weird . . . I was actually having fun.

OKAY, SO I DON'T ENTIRELY THINK YOU GUYS ARE GOING TO GET THIS, BUT TODAY WAS KIND OF A BIG DEAL FOR ME. COACH GAVE ME A JERSEY FOR THE TOURNEY TEAM. I AM OFFICIALLY A MEMBER OF **THE AURADON PREP FIGHTING KNIGHTS.** I DON'T KNOW WHY, BUT WHEN I WAS HOLDING THAT JERSEY IN MY HANDS, I WAS KIND OF EXCITED. COACH AND I TALKED ABOUT WHAT IT WOULD BE LIKE TO BE ON A TEAM, AND HOW A TEAM IS LIKE A FAMILY AND WE ALL WORK TOGETHER AND STUFF. IT WAS JUST COOL TO BE PART OF SOMETHING BIGGER THAN ME, YOU KNOW? HE THINKS I'M REALLY GOOD AT TOURNEY. EVERYONE DOES. AND THAT FEELS KIND OF . . . WELL,

AWESOME.

That's awesome, Jay.

GO, YOU!

How to Charm a Bat

The magickal charm of thine eye
Guide me this night.
Be mine consort,
Give me the gift of thine
Second sight.
By the old ones
May my will be done.

Do you guys think I should try to do Chad's homework in his handwriting, like match it? Or do you think it's okay if it's in mine?

The Look of Evil

If you harbor darkness in your heart,
There are ways to look,
Ways to be.

The skin should be covered with a rich powder.
Dark brows, arched at a high angle.
Purple-red lips. GOOD TIP...

Hair of black, purple, or blue,
Long fingernails painted with polish,
And clothes of the finest cloth.

IT'S NOT OKAY.

None of this is. Erie, you shouldn't be doing Chad's homework for him. He's just using you. What are you getting out of this? Where does he get off telling you to do his Chem homework for him? And why are you actually doing it?!?

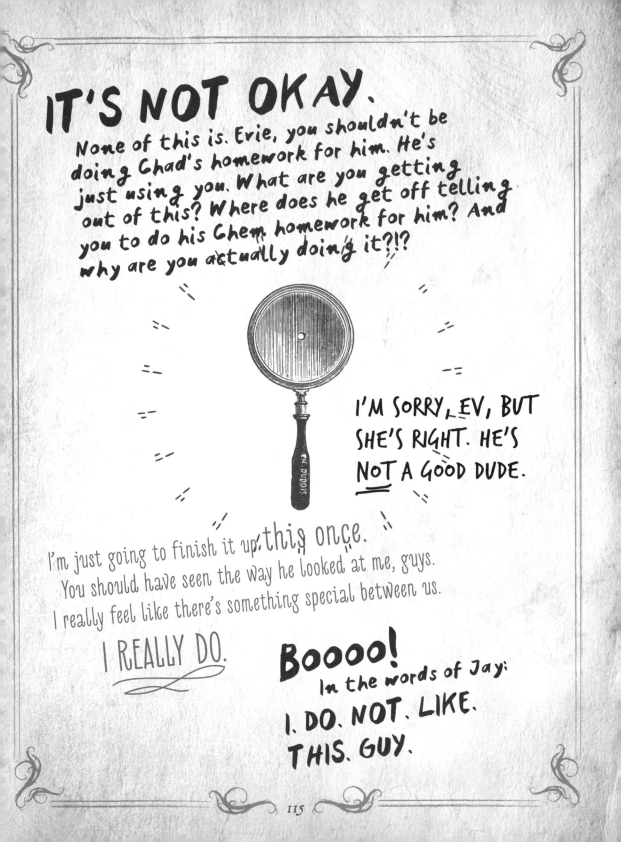

I'M SORRY, LEV, BUT SHE'S RIGHT. HE'S NOT A GOOD DUDE.

I'm just going to finish it up this once.
You should have seen the way he looked at me, guys.
I really feel like there's something special between us.

I REALLY DO.

BOOOO!
In the words of Jay:
I. DO. NOT. LIKE. THIS. GUY.

Okay, I know you're
busy being Chad's HOMEWORK SLAVE,
Evie; and I know you've been pretty psyched
about TOURNEY, Jay; and that you've been
busy practicing with Ben, Carlos.

But seriously. I have to point out there's been ZERO progress on getting the Fairy Godmother's magic wand.

Now that the plan with Jane is off, we need
to figure something else out, and I seriously
need you guys' help. No more slacking
off. I can't go back to the Isle of the Lost
without that wand. Maybe your parents
will let you come home, but my mom
definitely won't.

FAILURE IS NOT <u>AN</u> OPTION.

YOU'RE RIGHT,
MAL, WE HAVE BEEN SLACKING IN THE WHOLE
GET-THE-MAGIC-WAND-AND-TAKE-OVER-
AURADON DEPARTMENT. BUT IT'S NOT JUST YOU.
WE'RE ALL IN TROUBLE IF WE FAIL.
I'LL BE MORE OF A HELP... PINKIE-FINGER
PROMISE SWEAR

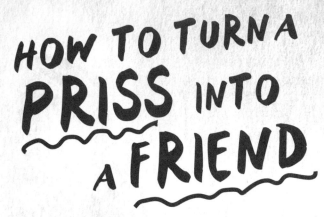

HOW TO TURN A PRISS INTO A FRIEND

1) Offer the priss something no one else can. A spell-driven makeover, a funky nail polish to borrow, or your punk music from the Isle of the Lost to listen to. She'll start to appreciate having a **DIFFERENT PERSPECTIVE.**

2) Invite the priss to join in something fun or just to hang out with you and your friends. If she feels included, she'll be more comfortable, and it'll be easier to get to know her.

3) Talk to the girl about something that's important to her, like her family, her friends, or her boyfriend. When you learn more about her, you may like her more.

4) What can you learn from this girl that you didn't know before? What can she teach you? For example, Lonnie taught us how to make rings out of paper clips. That was **KIND OF COOL.**

EVIE!!
You knew about the wand and the coronation all along!! I can't believe you didn't tell us sooner!!

I'M SORRY, GUYS.

It just slipped my mind. I was so caught up in doing Chad's homework I forgot that I saw Doug right after I left the bleachers, and he mentioned that Fairy Godmother uses the wand during Ben's coronation ceremony to bless him or something. The whole school attends the ceremony. If we can get there, we can get the wand. We just have to be in grabbing distance. **Hold that thought.**

☆ Love Spell ☆

Crush his heart with an iron glove
By making him a slave to love.
He'll have to eat
A sweet little treat
Made with the contents of one's soul.
Mix the following in a large iron bowl:
1 cup of butter churned by a young maiden
3/4 cup sugar
3/4 cup packed brown sugar
1 teaspoon of vanilla extract **??**
1 tear of human sadness
2 eggs from a black hen

AND LOTS OF CHOCOLATE CHIPS. YUM!!!

So we've confirmed that, yes, the magic wand is in fact used at the coronation ceremony, just like Doug, Dopey's son, claimed. Were you guys listening to what Ben said when he stopped by our room before? The only people allowed in the front row in the cathedral are his parents, him, and his GIRLFRIEND.
And maybe at first that might seem like a problem, but it's really not. Because Audrey might be his girlfriend right now, this second, but that's nothing a quick love spell can't fix.

In a bowl of marble, mix:

2 1/4 cups flour

1 teaspoon salt

A longing for love unending and pure

Memories of a happy time

1 teaspoon baking soda

When you've mixed these bowls up

Good and well,

Get ready to cast your lovesick spell.

Pour the contents of the marble bowl

Into the creamy batter

And turn twenty times while you incant:

GOOD IDEA, MAL.

IF YOU'RE IN THE FRONT ROW DURING THE CORONATION, WE MIGHT ACTUALLY BE ABLE TO PULL THIS OFF.

I can picture it: We're sitting there, watching Ben kneel in front of a huge crowd, when the Fairy Godmother steps forward. She pulls out her magic wand and brings it down, about to tap his shoulder, when Mal springs up from her seat in the front row and—YANK!—snatches the wand from FG's hand. The wand explodes with light. Magic ripples through the air. Everyone in the crowd gasps, watching as our friend Mal wields the wand, feeling her power for the first time and—

TAKE HIS HEART

AND LAY IT AT MY FEET.

FILL HIM WITH A SENSE OF AWE

FOR STRENGTH AND BEAUTY AND PROMISE

UNDER THE CONSTELLATION OF ORION AND

THE STAR PROCYON.

BREATHE LOVE INTO HIM, ALOFT THE

MOMENTTHIS BISCUIT BECOMES HIM,

MOVING PAST HIS PARTED LIPS.

Form into biscuits and bake ten turns of a minute Hourglass, in an oven heated to 376 degrees.

Okay, Evie. Points for enthusiasm!
But first, before any of that can happen, we need to find one tear of human sadness. I can't even remember the last time I cried. Maybe when I was a baby? Like fourteen years ago or something? What about you guys?

THE SADDEST THINGS THAT HAVE EVER HAPPENED TO ME

- One time I got caught manipulating my mom and she sent me to my room for three days straight. She would slide food under the door, and she stopped talking to me. I wasn't exactly sad, though, just lonely. But whatever. I never cry.

-BEFORE WE LEFT THE ISLE OF THE LOST, I GOT CAUGHT STEALING FROM ARTEM'S STORE AND HE THREATENED TO FILE CHARGES AGAINST ME. BUT I WASN'T REALLY SAD-MORE SCARED, I GUESS, BECAUSE THEN I WOULD HAVE TO STOP STEALING AND IT PROBABLY WOULD'VE COST MY DAD A TON OF GOLD TO GET ME OUT OF TROUBLE.

— Growing up I had a doll that I'd made out of rags. I named her Jocelyn. I sewed dresses for her and took her everywhere with me, but then one day a vulture ate her.

-A LOT OF SAD STUFF HAPPENED TO ME. I DON'T GET UPSET ABOUT IT, THOUGH, OR CRY ABOUT IT.
I GUESS I JUST TRY TO FORGET.
(AND WRITING ABOUT IT HERE ISN'T GOING TO HELP.)

SIDE NOTE: THAT LONNIE GIRL WHO WALKED IN WHILE WE WERE MIXING THE BATTER FOR THE LOVE SPELL— WHAT'S HER STORY?

♡ ♡

Someone has a crush!

Lost-and-Found Spell

An object gone missing,
It causes great strife.
Nothing is more
Troublesome in life.

So set out these items,
So near and dear,
And whisper above them
When the moment draws near.

The best thing about Lonnie is that her tear helped us complete the love spell. Now I have the perfect chocolate chip cookies to give to Ben to make him fall hopelessly in love with me. As soon as he takes a bite, then looks into my eyes, he'll be mine. Evie, do you want to start making my coronation gown?

I'M STILL THINKING ABOUT WHAT LONNIE SAID, THOUGH: THAT STORY SHE TOLD ABOUT HER MOM MAKING HER CHOCOLATE CHIP COOKIES WHEN SHE WAS SAD, AND TALKING TO HER, TELLING HER SHE CARED? THEN WHEN WE SAID WE DIDN'T GET WHAT SHE WAS TALKING ABOUT, SHE LOOKED AT US ALL TEARY-EYED. I THOUGHT EVEN VILLAINS LOVE THEIR KIDS.

I KNOW, JAY. I keep thinking about that, too. It's been bumming me out. I mean, I know my relationship with my mom isn't perfect, but when Lonnie was talking about her parents and how great they were . . . I just felt awful. Is that really what we've been missing?

5 gardenia petals
2 tears of human grief
A beloved object
The breath of a fairy
Skin of a newt
Whisper these words
So soft and true.
Then wait for your possession
To return to you.

WHAT HAS BEEN LOST
CAN STILL BE FOUND.
RISE, ALL THE SPIRITS
FROM THE COLD GROUND.
YOUR HELP IS NEEDED
WHEN SEARCHING ROUND.

It's just different where we come from. None of these kids can understand what it was like to grow up on the Isle of the Lost. Our parents raised us right, and that meant ignoring us a lot of the time and not catering to our every need. I don't know, I guess they thought it would make us stronger and tougher. Maybe it did.

YEAH, LONNIE JUST DOESN'T GET IT, THAT'S ALL. WE SHOULDN'T FEEL BAD ABOUT OUR PARENTS. HEROES JUST OPERATE DIFFERENTLY, YOU KNOW?

JAY! What was that moment of weakness about?!?! You guys, get this: I am walking toward Ben, the love spell cookie in my hand, getting ready to give it to him, and Jay looks at me and is like,

"Mal ... are you SURE you want to do this?! It's not like this is the unhappiest place on earth...."

HOW'S THAT FOR SECOND-GUESSING THE PLAN?!?

I KNOW, I KNOW! I JUST GOT CAUGHT UP IN MY HEAD AND STARTED OVERTHINKING IT. BUT NOW I'M BACK, GUYS.
LONG LIVE EVIL!
I'M BAD AND MEAN AND TERRIBLE!

Wands and Scepters

Wands and scepters are instruments of power,
Drivers of an unending force.
In your grasp they can split open the sky,
Explode stars, and break apart mountains.

Choose your instrument wisely.
Balsam fir, chopped from a tree
Rooted on a line of power,
Marble and crystal accoutrements,
Gold blessed by a hundred fairies—
All make fine components
Of a wand or a scepter.

That's more like it.
So, if any of you doubted this spell book before,
you saw what happened when I gave
Ben the cookie today. One bite and he was a
completely different person. Did you see the
way he was staring at me all googly-eyed?!

Dragons' Wings

Dragons' Wings are an

Invaluable ingredient for Spells.

Rare and precious,

The scales have healing properties

And the flesh has been known

To restore Strength if boiled in

Crow's blood and eaten off the bone.

His heart's all aflutter,
His brain's turned to butter,
His forehead is bathed in sweat.

MY FAVORITE PART WAS WHEN HE TRIED TO KISS MAL AND SHE BROUGHT UP HER HAND AND BLOCKED HIM. DID YOU SEE HIS FACE? IT'S LIKE HE LOVED HER EVEN MORE IN THAT MOMENT, LIKE HE WAS JUST FREAKING THRILLED.

WHENEVER HE'S NEAR HER,
  HIS LIFE BECOMES CLEARER.
HE KNOWS WHAT HE'S LIVING FOR.

I have to admit, I loved when Ben was like, "Mal, will you be my girlfriend?" The look on Audrey's face was great. I wasn't so fond of the part when Audrey laid claim to Chad, kissed him, and said he was her date to the coronation. But at least it got us what we wanted: Ben taking Mal to the coronation.

DID BEN MENTION THAT HE'S IN LOVE WITH MAL?

Haha. Only about a HUNDRED TIMES.
When is a boy going to say that about me?

There's always that cookie recipe. . . .
  Oh, I forgot, you're a romantic, Evie,
and you probably want "true love."
          BLECH.

Symbols and Meanings of Totem Animals

An animal seen in a moment
Can provide clarity and meaning.

To interpret the signs and symbols of
Animal totems, use this guide.

WE KILLED THE SHERWOOD FALCONS TODAY!
I KNOW I'M SUPPOSED TO BE WORRIED ABOUT THE WAND
AND OUR PLAN AND STUFF, BUT SERIOUSLY, WHEN I'M
OUT ON THE TOURNEY FIELD, IT'S LIKE EVERYTHING ELSE
FALLS AWAY. DID YOU GUYS SEE CARLOS'S BIG PLAY?!? HE
WAS THE STAR OF THE GAME. WHEN THAT PLAYER
CHECKED ME, I THOUGHT FOR SURE WE'D LOST THE BALL,
THAT IT WAS GOING TO HIT THE TURF AND IT'D BE OVER,
NO POINTS FOR US. BUT THEN CARLOS DIVED FORWARD
AND GRABBED IT JUST BEFORE IT DROPPED. THEN HE
PASSED IT TO BEN, AND THEN: SCORE!!!

It was pretty incredible, C. We're proud of you!

You zigzagged across the field like it was nothing—two yards, then another two, then six. All that training with Ben and Dude has really paid off.

Dolphin: harmony, playfulness, and cooperation

Panda: gentle strength, nurturing

Hummingbird: joy, lightness of being, love

Crow: clairvoyance, change, ancient wisdom

Beaver: problem solving, cooperation

Bear: vision quest, meditation

Fox: charm, curiosity, luck

Hawk: fearlessness, intensity

Wolf: self-reliance, intelligence

THAT WAS SERIOUSLY AWESOME.

DID YOU SEE HOW JAY PUT ME ON HIS SHOULDERS? THE WHOLE TEAM WAS CHEST BUMPING AND HIGH-FIVING ME. IT WAS LIKE . . . ONE OF THE BEST DAYS OF MY LIFE.

WHEN YOU HELPED BEN SCORE THAT GOAL, YOU GROWLED LIKE A DOG, CARLOS! WE HAVE TO START CALLING YOU THE ANIMAL, BECAUSE YOU TEAR EVERYONE APART. HOW'S THAT FOR A NICKNAME?

Penguin: duty, survival, elegance

Deer: adventure, innocence

Horse: freedom, endurance

Elephant: strength, patience

Bat: trust, swiftness

Lion: wisdom, strength

Butterfly: freedom, transcendence, grace

Leopard: secrets, mystery

I'm so impressed, C! I only wish I wasn't so distracted by all of Ben's craziness. Seriously, when he grabbed the megaphone and started spelling out my name with the entire crowd? How he kept yelling about how R-I-D-I-C-U-L-O-U-S our love is? I just wanted to crawl into a hole.

Gimme an M. . . .
Gimme an A. . . .
Gimme an L. . . .

Come on, Mal.
It's hard for me to feel too sorry for you. A prince is in love with you. And Audrey got so mad at Ben for singing that song in front of everyone that she told him she wasn't going to the coronation with him anymore. Now he's your date, and you'll be right there when FG takes out her magic wand. It's a win-win.

Peacock: self-expression, prosperity

Porcupine: nonchalance, self-protection

Polar bear: surrender, acceptance

Skunk: respect, clarity

Snake: healing, light energy

Whale: song, ritual, intuition

I'm sorry, Evie. You're right, I shouldn't be complaining—not after what happened today with Chad. Who would've thought Audrey would choose him, out of all princes, to rebound with??
   If it makes you feel any better, I don't think she actually likes him, and even if she did, it won't be long before he realizes how awful she is.
   I GIVE THEM A WEEK, TOPS.

Those Entitled to Respect

Maleficent

Mother Gothel

The Evil Queen

Shan-yu

Claude Frollo

Lady Tremaine

Jafar

Chernabog

Governor Ratcliffe

Madame Medusa

Ursula the sea Witch

Gaston

Scar

Stromboli

Big Bad Wolf

Aunt Sarah

Prince John

Hades

Cruella De Vil

Captain Hook

Amos Slade

Kaa

Shere Khan

I just . . . It's not like Chad has no say in it. He could've told her he was dating someone, or he wanted to ask someone else to the coronation, or he just didn't want to be her boyfriend. It's just . . . I don't know what I did wrong. I did all his homework for him, just like he asked me to. And I wore all my cutest clothes the past week and did my hair and tried to be charming and aloof . . . I just . . . I don't know.

YOU DIDN'T DO ANYTHING WRONG, EVIE. **YOU'RE PERFECT.** CHAD IS THE ONE WHO NEEDS TO RETHINK THINGS. YOU WERE ALWAYS BETTER THAN HIM. YOU'RE SMART AND FUNNY AND VERY, VERY COOL. DON'T GET DOWN ON YOURSELF JUST BECAUSE THIS ONE IDIOT CAN'T SEE HOW GREAT YOU ARE. WE ALL SEE IT. WE KNOW.

JAY'S RIGHT. YOU'RE SO MUCH BETTER THAN HIM, EVIE! IT'S TIME YOU SEE THAT. WHO CARES WHAT CHAD THINKS? HE'S JUST SOME PRINCE IN SOME STUFFY CASTLE. HE'S OBVIOUSLY MISSING OUT ON A GOOD THING.

And just a reminder: after the coronation we'll be done with this place. We'll be back on the Isle of the Lost with the magic wand, and all of Auradon will be ours. Chad will be a **DISTANT MEMORY.**

Guys . . . today was the worst day ever.

I'm not even exaggerating. Remember how I told you I've been using my magic mirror in Chem class to get the answers? Well, we had a test today, and I had it in my purse. I was looking down every now and then to see the equations, and then Mr. Delay caught me. Apparently Chad told him I'd been cheating with the mirror.

As if it's not bad enough that Chad totally used me to do his homework. As if it doesn't hurt that he's dating Audrey. Now he's trying to get me expelled from school. Seriously, if it wasn't for Doug, Mr. Delay would have just thrown me out right there. Doug argued with him and got me a second chance. I took the test by myself, without the mirror, and got a B+. I'm still here . . . for now.

DID I MENTION I HATE THIS KID?!?
WHEN WE WERE ON THE TOURNEY FIELD, PLAYING THE FALCONS, I HAD A MINUTE WHERE I THOUGHT HE ACTUALLY MIGHT BE OKAY. BUT THEN HE DOES THIS. IT MAKES ME SO MAD I WANT TO PUNCH SOMETHING.

CAN WE ALL AGREE THAT DOUG IS GREAT? THAT HE'S GENUINE AND KIND AND LOOKS OUT FOR EVERYONE, NO MATTER WHO THEY ARE? HE'S REALLY THE NICEST PERSON I'VE MET AT AURADON, WITH THE EXCEPTION OF THE LOVE OF MAL'S LIFE, AKA BEN.

very funny, C.

The Most Reviled Do-Gooders

Fairy Godmother

Ariel

Peter Pan

~~Cinderella~~

~~Prince Charming~~

Rapunzel

Li Shang

Quasimodo

Pongo

Perdita

Snow White

Belle

Hercules

Pocahontas

Jasmine

Tiana

Prince Eric

Maid Marian

Robin Hood

Beast

Mulan

Aladdin

See, Evie?!?! The spell book says his parents are "reviled." Good riddance.

I'm sorry, Evie—and you know how I feel about Chad. Maybe this will be the thing that finally makes you not like him?

A Chant for Strength

FILL ME UP,

Make me strong,

ALL the power of the ages

That has come and gone.

GIVE IT TO ME,

Make it right,

After the third sun rises

And that day slips into night.

YOU DEFINITELY COULD. :)

I guess if anything good came out of this, it's that I got a B+ and I didn't even try. That was with zero studying and barely paying attention in class. Maybe if I actually put some effort in, I could get an A.

SO, MAL. HEARD YOU HAD A BIG DATE LAST NIGHT WITH PRINCE BEN. THIS WHOLE "WE'RE! IN! LOVE!" ACT IS GETTING PRETTY COMPLICATED, HUH? I HOPE YOU WERE ABLE TO KEEP YOUR DINNER DOWN.

I get credit for her makeup!

FILL ME UP,

Make me strong,

ALL the power of the ages

That has come and gone.

It was actually kind of . . . cool. I mean, it could be worse, you know? He picked me up on his Vespa and we took all these roads out to the Enchanted Lake. (No, it's nothing like the Enchanted Lake in Journey into the Enchanted Forest. Don't even ask.) We had a picnic and went swimming (or he went swimming; I almost drowned). It was really . . . nice. Fun.

GIVE IT TO ME,

Make it right,

After the third sun rises

And that day slips into night.

DID MAL, ONLY DAUGHTER OF MALEFICENT, JUST USE THE WORD NICE?!?!

Carlos's Magical Recipe for Conquering Your Fears

/ / / / / / / / / /

Step One:
Recognize that you're afraid of something, like dogs (just an example). Don't pretend like you're not afraid or make excuses for how you feel. Just say it out loud:
"I am afraid of dogs."

Step Two:
Whatever you're afraid of, face it head-on. It helps to have a friend with you when you do this, because it can be pretty scary. Like if you're afraid of dogs (again, just an example), let a dog lick your face. Even if you're scared, just let it happen.

Step Three:
Stay calm, no matter how afraid you are. The fear will pass. When it does, you will be stronger. Every time you're in a situation with a dog, you'll feel even better about being there. After a while you won't be afraid at all.

We're so proud of you, Carlos!

More details about the date, please!
What did he say? Did you kiss?

No kissing. Definitely not.
I don't know ... he said a lot of things. He
said he loved me (for like the millionth time).
Apparently the spell is still really strong.
He said he's excited about the coronation
and he has this whole speech planned. He's
going to talk about us and how we make
our own choices, and how we're not our
parents and blah blah blah.

LITTLE DOES HE KNOW WE'RE
PLOTTING TO STEAL THE WAND
AND **TAKE OVER AURADON**.

BEN'S RIGHT, THOUGH.
WE'RE NOT OUR PARENTS.
I'M NOTHING LIKE MY MOM.

I have to give Ben credit—
his optimism is contagious.

How to Raise Evil Spawn

Do tell them they're not good enough.
Do put pressure on them to succeed.
Do stress the importance of being evil.

Don't feed them with any regularity.
Don't give them a warm place to sleep at night.
Don't give them clean clothes to wear.

Always turn your back on them when they try to hug you.
Always humiliate them in front of their friends.
Always tell them how powerful you are.

Never tuck them in at night.
Never tell them you love them.
Never kiss their owies.*

* BY KISSING A WOUND, YOU DRAW THE
WEAKNESS INTO YOURSELF.
DO THIS FOR NO ONE.

WOW. FAMILY DAY.
EVEN THOUGH WE ONLY HAD TO "VISIT" WITH OUR PARENTS ON VIDEO CHAT, IT WAS STILL TERRIBLE. THERE'S A TRADITION I COULD DO AWAY WITH.

I know, it was TORTURE. And the way they were arguing with each other . . . so embarrassing. Did you see my mom?!? She kept looking at herself in the bottom of the screen, like it was a mirror. I know Fairy Godmother wanted us to have some kind of Family Day, even though our parents can't come to Auradon for, well, OBVIOUS reasons, but it was kind of hard to talk to my mom, even if it was just a video call. I kept wondering what she would say about Chad and thinking about how she'd probably think I'm a failure and how she'd never like Doug, since he's just the son of a dwarf.

I KNOW WHAT YOU MEAN, EV.
DID YOU NOTICE MY MOM'S FACE WHEN SHE SAW DUDE IN MY ARMS? SHE WANTED TO COME THROUGH THE SCREEN, GRAB HIM, AND TURN HIM INTO SOME EARMUFFS.

Random question . . .
what's with her dog stole??

NO. CLUE.

THAT WAS UNBEARABLE.

Every other word out of my mom's mouth was about how she MUST see the wand soon, how she HAS TO get her hands on it, how she doesn't know what she'll do without it. Yes, she was speaking in code in front of Fairy Godmother, but still. If we don't succeed with this plan . . . we can't go back to the Isle of the Lost. I won't be able to face her, not after all this.

WE'RE ALL IN THIS TOGETHER, MAL.

THERE'S NO WAY MY MOM IS GOING TO LET ME BRING DUDE BACK TO THE ISLAND, SO WE HAVE TO TAKE OVER AURADON. I CAN'T SAY GOOD-BYE TO HIM NOW. LET'S GO OVER THE PLAN ONE MORE TIME. WHILE YOU'RE INSIDE AT THE CORONATION, JAY WILL KEEP WATCH ON THE BALCONY. THEN I'LL FIND THE LIMO OUTSIDE SO THAT EVIE CAN KNOCK THE DRIVER OUT WITH THE ATOMIZER. THEN, ONCE YOU HAVE THE WAND, YOU AND JAY WILL RUN TO THE LIMO AND WE'LL TAKE OFF, BACK THE WAY WE CAME, OVER THE SECRET BRIDGE TO THE ISLE OF THE LOST.

The Hero's Dilemma

The hero will fight valiantly.
Sword in hand, he will face off
Against the villain, ready to
Bring the moment to a crisis.
He lives by his ideals—
A code of honor never broken,
A desire to help others.
On this battlefield, the one
Staged between hero and villain,
His goodness will not serve him.
Wait for the moment of weakness,
For a softening of his temperament.
Use his empathy against him
And his life will be your reward.

I SHOULD KEEP THIS FOR HEROISM CLASS.

Exactly. Remember, Erie, just **TWO SPRAYS** with the atomizer should be enough to knock the driver out. Don't go overboard.

Roger that.

COOL. SO WE HAVE A PLAN.
IN JUST A FEW DAYS WE'LL HAVE THE WAND. THEN WE'LL BE AWAY FROM AURADON FOREVER—WHICH IS A GOOD THING, RIGHT?

I KNOW THIS MIGHT SOUND WEAK, BUT I'M GOING TO MISS PLAYING TOURNEY HERE. I MEAN, WHEN THE CANNONS START FIRING AND YOU'RE RACING UP THE FIELD, PLAYERS COMING AT YOU FROM ALL DIRECTIONS . . . THERE'S NO BETTER FEELING THAN THAT.

IT'LL JUST BE SAD, MAYBE . . .
TO LEAVE THAT BEHIND.

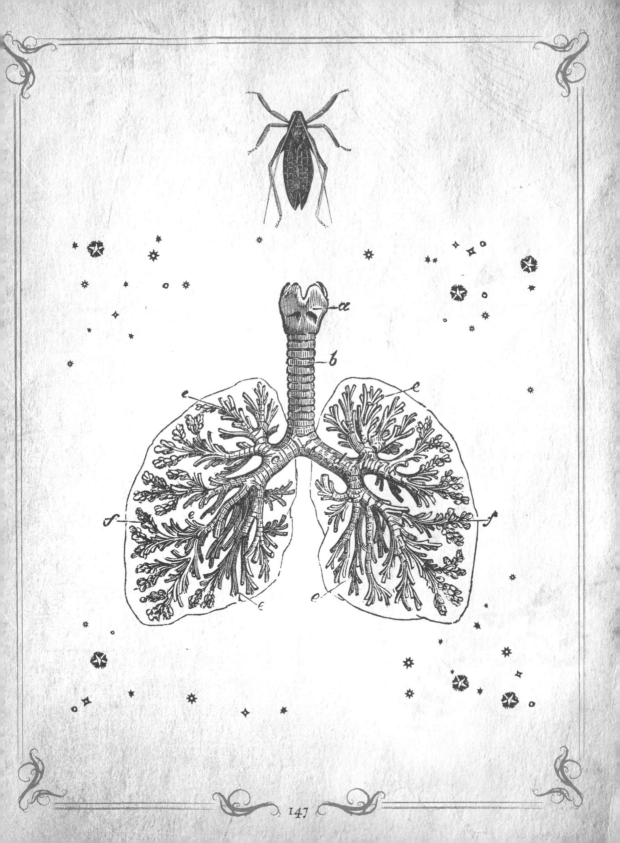

Flowers with Power

These flowers are known for
Their potency. Because they are used in
Various Potions and Spells, it is wise to look
For them and collect them in copious amounts
Whenever traveling through the wood.

I KNOW WHAT YOU MEAN, JAY. I GUESS I WAS
THINKING THAT DUDE WOULD STAY HERE, IN AURADON,
UNTIL I COULD COME BACK. BUT WHO'S GOING TO TAKE
CARE OF HIM? I MEAN, I HANG OUT WITH THE LITTLE GUY
EVERY DAY. I'M THE ONE WHO GIVES HIM CHICKEN
AND FRIED RICE FROM THE CAFETERIA. I'M THE ONE
WHO TAKES HIM ON LONG WALKS, GIVES HIM BELLY RUBS,
AND THROWS THE BALL FOR HIM. I GUESS I SHOULD ASK
SOMEONE ELSE TO, BUT I'M JUST WORRIED THAT DUDE
WON'T BE SAFE ONCE WE TAKE THE WAND.

Amaryllis

Aster

Calla

Chrysanthemum

Cymbidium

Gardenia

Freesia

Heliconia

Lily of the valley

Spray rose

Statice

Stock

Waxflower

I guess that B+ is the first and last one I'll ever get. There's no way I'm going back to school on the Isle of the Lost. That place was chaos. Fights all the time, teachers who didn't care about us, people stealing your books and your wallet whenever you weren't looking. I even had my gym clothes stolen once . . . GROSS.

I know . . . it's going to be hard not to see Ben anymore. Like, one day he's my boyfriend and I hang out with him all the time; then the next I'm **BETRAYING HIS COUNTRY AND NEVER SEEING HIM AGAIN**. It's more than a little weird. It's just . . . this is what we have to do. We can't go back to the Isle of the Lost without the wand.

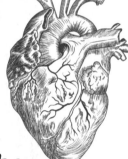

DO WE HAVE TO GO BACK AT ALL?

We have to.
We can't go back on the plan now. Look, I'm going to make a cupcake tonight to break the love spell, one that I can give Ben before the coronation. I figure it's cruel to not only take over Ben's future kingdom, but leave him hopelessly in love with me. But then that's it. We'll go to the silly celebration tomorrow for Auradon Family Day, then the coronation. Then we'll leave. We have to bring back the wand. . . . **WE DON'T HAVE A CHOICE.**

How to Break a Love Spell

This heart I bound

With my dark Spell,

But everything's
a choice—
isn't that what
Fairy Godmother says?

Set it free and make

It well.

NOT THIS.

Break the chains that make

It mine

So that true love's light

May shine.

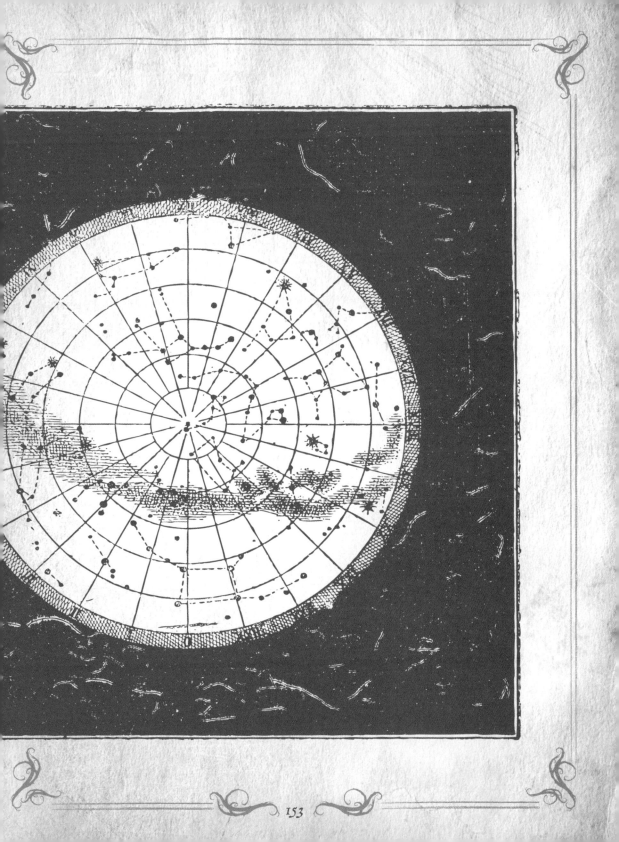

Fairy Tales for the Young

The Giant's Death

A giant once lived in a house in the clouds.

He was there, minding his own business,

When a little boy named Jack broke in.

The giant had a keen sense of smell

And sensed something was wrong.

Still, the boy was able to make off

With a bag of gold coins.

That wasn't enough, apparently, because the

Boy came back for a goose that laid golden eggs.

He took that; then he took a harp that played by itself.

Guys . . . I'm SO, SO SORRY I messed up Family
Day. I was trying to help Jay, and I didn't know what to
do. When Chad and Jay started fighting, I just pulled out
the atomizer and sprayed Chad. It seemed like a good idea at
the time—the only way to stop Chad from hitting Jay.

After the third robbery, the giant chased

Jack out of the clouds,

But he fell and was killed.

If only the giant had found the boy sooner. If only he had followed

Him down into the town below and stepped on Jack's house

With his heavy giant's foot.

AND EVERYONE
THINKS I'M THE HOTHEAD. If only.
WHAT WERE YOU THINKING,
TAKING OUT THE ATOMIZER AT FAMILY DAY, IN
FRONT OF HUNDREDS OF AURADON PREP STUDENTS
AND THEIR PARENTS?! NOW EVERYONE KNOWS WE'VE
BEEN USING MAGIC. **WE'RE TOTAL OUTCASTS.**
WE HAD TO RUN OFF THE QUAD LIKE DUNGEON ESCAPEES.

YEAH, BUT LET'S FACE IT.
WE WERE ALWAYS OUTCASTS.
AS SOON AS WE WALKED ONTO THAT QUAD THIS
MORNING, EVERYONE WAS STARING AT US, WONDERING
WHY WE WERE THE ONLY STUDENTS WHOSE PARENTS
WEREN'T THERE. WE EVEN DRESS DIFFERENTLY FROM
THE AURADON KIDS. NO MATTER HOW PREPPY WE TRY
TO BE, WE'LL NEVER FIT IN.

The Big Bad Wolf

There once was a powerful and courageous
Wolf, who roamed the dark depths of
The forest. He was evil and mean, with horrible
Fangs and breath that smelled of dead
Squirrels. In the woods he found three houses,
One of straw, one of wood, and one of bricks.
Each held a fat, self-righteous little pig.

This isn't Evie's fault, it's **Queen Leah's.** I was just walking through the crowd, looking for you guys, when she came up to me. You should have seen the way she looked at me. Her nose was all scrunched up, like she got a whiff of rotting garbage. Then she started yelling as if I were my mother. She started telling everyone that I was no good, and that Ben was foolish for letting us into Auradon. I mean . . . what's the point in being better when no one cares?!? People are always going to see us as our parents' kids. **Nothing we can do will change that.**

I wish Chad hadn't even been there today. When he heard Queen Leah . . . then he joined in . . . UGH. It makes my stomach hurt. Was what he said true? Am I just a gold digger and a cheater?

THAT'S NOT TRUE, EVIE–NONE OF IT IS. I'M NOT JUST A THIEF. MAL ISN'T JUST A GIRL WHO STOLE SOMEONE ELSE'S BOYFRIEND. THERE'S SO MUCH MORE TO US THAN THAT. AND I KNOW MAL'S RIGHT, IT ISN'T YOUR FAULT–I'M SORRY. I SHOULDN'T HAVE PUSHED CHAD TO BEGIN WITH. IT'S JUST WHEN I HEARD HIM CALLING YOU THOSE NAMES . . . IT WASN'T RIGHT. I KIND OF SNAPPED.

The first two houses he blew down with one breath,

killing the pigs inside. The third was too sturdy

To be knocked down, so the wolf climbed through

The window, killed the pig, and ate him.

Pork had never tasted so good.

Guys . . . I hate it here now. Today, what happened at the picnic benches?!? Audrey and all her friends were laughing at us. We're a joke to them, just some villains' kids who shouldn't be here. Just a few more days until the coronation–that's what I keep telling myself.
Then we blow this Popsicle stand.

At least you got back at Jane by undoing her hair spell, Mal. She can't make fun of us and also benefit from your magic. That doesn't seem fair.

Nobody talked to me in Heroism today. Nobody talked to me in Basic Chivalry, either. They all just looked right past me and Jay like we weren't even there. This whole thing just makes me want to crawl in bed with Dude and not come out until the coronation. Dogs are amazing, because they never judge you.

WE'RE NOT AS BAD AS THEY SAY WE ARE . . . RIGHT?

WE'RE DEFINITELY NOT. AND WHO CARES WHAT THEY SAY? FINE, MAYBE ME, A LITTLE BIT. JUST A REALLY LITTLE BIT OF ME. BESIDES, AREN'T PEOPLE ALLOWED TO MAKE MISTAKES? DON'T YOU GUYS BELIEVE WHAT BEN SAID, THAT WE'RE ABLE TO CHANGE IF WE WANT TO? WHY DOES ANYONE ELSE GET TO DECIDE WHO WE ARE?

BEN. The one person who's still talking to us, even after the incident at Family Day. I guess we were right about one thing: he is a decent guy. He's been a friend to us, even if **no one else has.**

The Blind Witch

There was a mean, brutal old witch
Who lived in the middle of the forest in a
House she had painstakingly crafted out
Of gingerbread and sugar. She'd lived
An extraordinary life but was blind from all
The spells she'd cast. One morning she
Heard children laughing on her roof.
She went outside and realized a boy named Hansel
And his sister, Gretel, were eating her house.
She captured them and held them there
Until they eventually killed her by pushing her
Into her own oven. Then they left with all her gold.

THE MORAL OF THE STORY:
SHE SHOULD'VE KILLED THEM FIRST,
WHEN SHE HAD THE CHANCE.

Doug and Lonnie have been our friends, too . . .
they're just caught in the middle right now.

It's no excuse.

It's almost over. Only one more day until the coronation. No more walking down the halls alone, being ignored by everyone. No more having people get up and leave every time we sit down at their table at lunch. I am so over this place. It's terrible, and EVERYONE HERE IS TERRIBLE. (Okay, you're right, Mal—maybe not Ben. But one person isn't enough of a reason to stay.)

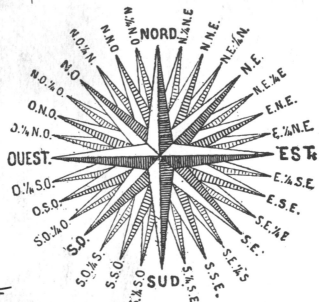

I'm getting sick thinking about how much it's going to kill Ben to know we betrayed him. I have to remind myself that he's only being kind to us because of the love spell. He's still in love with me, and he will be until he eats that cupcake before the coronation. He's nice to me because he's under a spell; he's nice to you guys because he's under a spell. . . . I have to remember that.

How to Tell If You're Being Used

∽ He (or she) only wants to spend time with you when you are doing something for him (or her).

∽ He constantly asks for favors, like doing his homework, carrying his books, or picking up his lunch.

∽ He never asks questions about your life, your friends, or your family.

∽ He shows little or no interest in meeting your friends.

∽ He's cold when you refuse to do something he asked.

Under the Sea

In the depths of the ocean there lived a miserable
little mermaid who cried all the time because
she wanted to go on land. A sea witch
named Ursula granted her that wish and was smart
And cunning. She took Ariel's voice as her
reward. When the little mermaid tried to mess with
Her, Ursula went on land and transformed into a beautiful
Woman. Then she stole the mermaid's boyfriend . . .
at least for a while.

I KEEP REMINDING MYSELF OF THAT, TOO, MAL. HE'S
UNDER A SPELL, RIGHT? THE DUDE WOULD DEFINITELY
NOT BE AS NICE TO US IF HE WASN'T IN LOVE WITH YOU.
IT'S ALL FAKE. . . .

I DON'T KNOW. BEN WAS ALWAYS PRETTY NICE TO ME, EVEN BEFORE MAL GAVE HIM THAT COOKIE. I THINK MAYBE HE'S JUST A GOOD PERSON? AND MAYBE IT'S HARD FOR US TO TELL BECAUSE WE'VE NEVER MET A GOOD PERSON BEFORE—LIKE A REALLY, TRULY GOOD PERSON?

The coronation is TOMORROW, Carlos. This is not helping! We have to do this. Tomorrow, Carlos, you will find the limo. Evie will use the atomizer to knock out the driver. Jay will provide backup while I steal the wand from the Fairy Godmother. Then we'll all return to Isle of the Lost. THE END.

THERE ARE SO MANY THINGS TO CELEBRATE I DON'T KNOW WHERE TO START.

First I guess I should tell you guys what happened on the carriage ride to the cathedral. I gave Ben the cupcake to eat, but he said he knew all about the love spell and that I was giving him the cupcake to break it. He told me he **HASN'T BEEN UNDER THE SPELL** since he went swimming in the Enchanted Lake, which was like . . . ages ago.

So you were right—we all were. He IS a nice guy. A kind, gentle, good-hearted person. Does that explain what happened a little bit? Why I decided at the last second not to use the wand for evil? If only my mother hadn't shown up. . . .

ALSO . . . a big thing to celebrate: everyone loved my coronation gown.

THANK YOU, EVIE!

You. Are. Welcome.

I think when the wand came out of the Fairy Godmother's hand, the barrier around the Isle of the Lost must've been weakened. How else would your mother have been able to get off the island and come to the cathedral? Her powers were back.

The Three Bears

There once was a cottage in the middle
Of the forest, where three bears lived together
In harmony. There was a large bear, a small
Bear, and one of medium size. They were out
One day, on a picnic, and when they returned,
They found the door to their cottage was open.
Someone had broken in. The porridge they'd
Left out had been eaten. Their kitchen was a
Mess. The smallest bear's favorite chair
Was broken, as if someone with a large
Bottom had squeezed himself into it.
Then they found a girl with tons of blond curls
Sleeping in the largest bear's bed. That was it.
They'd had enough. The largest bear ate the girl
For lunch, sharing her with the other two.

YOU GUYS ARE FUNNY. YOU'RE CELEBRATING THE
CORONATION DRESS FIRST?!? YES, I KNOW SNOW WHITE WAS RAAAAAAVING
ABOUT IT, BUT WE JUST DEFEATED YOUR MOTHER, MALEFICENT, ONE OF
THE MOST POWERFUL AND FRIGHTENING FAIRIES TO EVER FLY THROUGH
AURADON. NOW THAT IS A HUGE ACCOMPLISHMENT.

OTHER THINGS TO CELEBRATE: WE GET TO STAY IN AURADON, AWAY FROM OUR PARENTS.
    I GET TO KEEP DUDE.
PEOPLE SEE US AS HEROES NOW, NOT OUTCASTS WHO WILL NEVER CHANGE.

THOSE ARE ALL REALLY GOOD THINGS.

BEST THINGS ABOUT THE CORONATION CEREMONY

THE MOMENT WHEN EVERYONE BECAME UNFROZEN AND MALEFICENT'S SPELL WAS BROKEN.

After I DEFEATED MY MOTHER, Ben came to from the frozen spell and gave me a huge hug. He said something about how I had saved him, and I remember feeling really . . . HAPPY. For the first time in a long time.

Okay, Jay says I'm not allowed to talk about the coronation dress anymore, so I can't have that be one of my favorite moments (although I LOVED when you stepped out of the carriage, Mal, and everyone was oohing and aahing). I think my favorite moment was when we decided together to choose good.

DEFINITELY WHEN YOU SAVED ME FROM THE DRAGON, MAL. YOUR MOM HAD JUST TRANSFORMED INTO THE MASSIVE BEAST AND SHE WAS FOLLOWING ME, SWOOPING DOWN, ABOUT TO STRIKE. IF IT WASN'T FOR YOU, I MIGHT BE DEAD.

Healing Potion

If you're feeling sick,
This potion
Should do the trick
To make you feel healthy and strong.

Put the following in a cup,
Then stir it all up
While reciting this quick
Little song.

5 drops dragon's blood
Eye of a newt
Dust from a witch's broom
1 cup water from a river on a line of power

INFUSE THIS POTION WITH STRENGTH.
GIVE IT THE POWER TO HEAL ALL WOUNDS
AND CURE ALL DISEASE. NO MATTER THE SEVERITY.
RESTORE THE DRINKER'S CAPABILITIES.
MAKE HER HEALTHY AND STRONG.

Moments When You Thought You Were a Goner

When my mom came through the cathedral window in her glowing green orb. Seriously, I've never seen her so powerful. And I'VE NEVER BEEN SO SCARED IN MY ENTIRE LIFE.

MALEFICENT HAD ME CORNERED ON THE SIDE OF THE CATHEDRAL. I COULD **HEAR THE DRAGON BREATHING**, AND SHE WAS ABOUT TO SHOOT FIRE ALL OVER ME BEFORE MAL STEPPED IN.

WHEN MALEFICENT TRANSFORMED INTO A DRAGON, DEFINITELY. I DIDN'T EVEN KNOW SHE COULD DO THAT. SUPER SCARY

There was a moment when Mal almost tripped on the red carpet, and I thought: Noooo!! The dress!!

YOU'RE KIDDING, RIGHT?

YES. ☺

REAL GOODNESS
LIKE A CASTLE, REQUIRES:

* CONSTANT vigilance

* A bright flag, to let the world see who you are

* Space enough inside for all those who seek the SHELTER OF YOUR FRIENDSHIP

* A STRONG DOOR, through which only good influences may enter

* A FIRM FOUNDATION, without which goodness may crumble

* Plenty of windows, through which to let the LIGHT OF GOODNESS IN

* A high vantage point to watch out for trouble

If you choose good, you don't have enemies. LOVE CONQUERS ALL.

~~A Spell to Determine Thine Enemy~~

The celebration tonight was incredible. All of Auradon Prep was lit up in different colors. Everyone was so kind to us, even the people who haven't spoken to us for the past few weeks. I tried to practice forgiveness, like Fairy Godmother taught us. She said it's one of the most important virtues. I'm starting to think she was right about that . . . and maybe she was right about a lot of things.

The magus who flies by night is
Not to be trusted.

His words are empty vessels bereft
Of any substance.

He operates by sleight of hand.

To find his treacherous hierophant,
You must take (a scrying bowl)

And fill it half full with water

Drawn from a well that is sited
on a line of power.

Add two drops of dragon's blood
And essence of calendula,

Then by the hourglass await

A cycle and then gaze into the
Scrying pool.

Therein you shall
See the face of thine enemy.

Time's arrow has a
Straight shaft, as it must travel unwavering
Into the future, to the morrow.
Do not believe anyone who
Insists that there is a crook
In the middling part of that.
Such a wight is playing
You as a novice or a fool.
On time's pages the words are
Writ large, indelible and certain
With age, unalterable in and of
Themselves. The wise magus knows
Full well that time's effect can
Be made keen or rendered dull.
The magic is at the arrowhead—
This is where the magus can affect
His macrocosm and the world entire.

THIS IS WEIRD.
FOR THE FIRST
TIME IN MY ENTIRE
LIFE, I'M, LIKE,
POPULAR. DID YOU
SEE HOW MANY KIDS
WERE COMING UP TO
ME, CHATTING ABOUT
THE CORONATION OR
TOURNEY, OR JUST
TRYING TO MAKE
CONVERSATION?
IT'S KIND OF
FUNNY.

PS DOES ANYONE
KNOW WHAT A
SCRYING BOWL IS?
SERIOUSLY, WHAT
IS THAT?

PPS I have no idea.

DON'T LET IT
GO TO YOUR
HEAD, JAY.

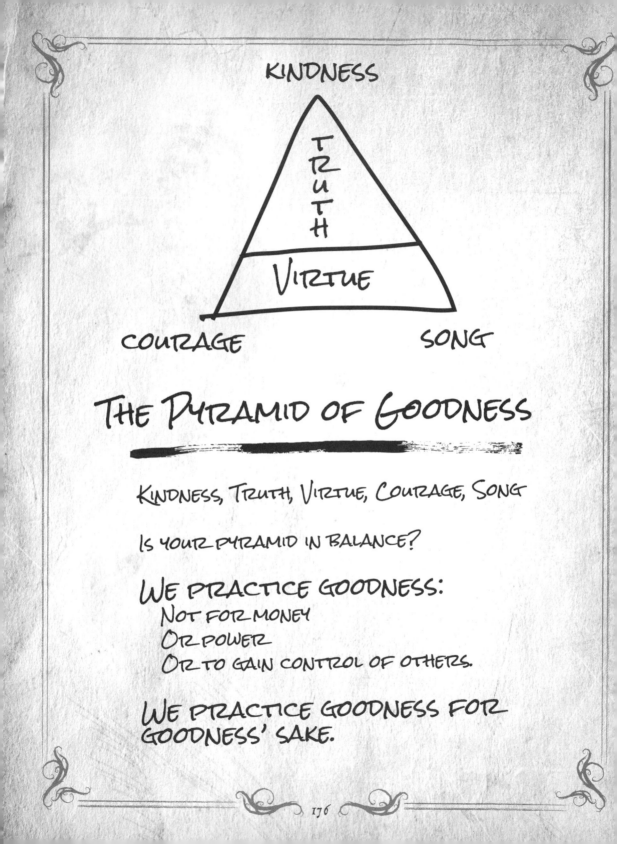

KINDNESS

TRUTH

VIRTUE

COURAGE   SONG

THE PYRAMID OF GOODNESS

Kindness, Truth, Virtue, Courage, Song

Is your pyramid in balance?

WE PRACTICE GOODNESS:
   Not for money
   Or power
   Or to gain control of others.

WE PRACTICE GOODNESS FOR GOODNESS' SAKE.

A Chant for the Brokenhearted

Stop the pain caused by love
I beg for help, sent from above

Let the light of healing in
Give me hope to begin again

Stop the pain caused by love
I beg for help, sent from above

Let the light of healing in
Give me hope to begin again

This is so strange . . .
I actually LIKE going
to school now.

Today, in Chemistry, I got an A- on the pop quiz Mr. Delay gave.
(For the record, that's three grades higher than Chad's.) Doug has
agreed to be my lab partner. Maybe he's just a dwarf's son, but
that's fine by me. I've never met anyone kinder in my whole
life. HE'S MORE OF A PRINCE THAN CHAD EVER WAS.

Poison Apples

Apples require a complicated poison
Brewed for twelve hours in a cast
Iron pot that once belonged to a
Female ogre. These pots can be
Nearly impossible to procure, so
They're often passed down through
Families for centuries.

Once found, mix 2 pounds of
Salamander skin and 3 drops
Vulture's blood together, Stirring for
Ten minutes in said pot. It's necessary to
Find a hog's hair to boil with the mixture.
Add gardenia extract and sugar to
Neutralize the taste, then simmer for twelve hours.
Paint the apple's skin with a thin coat
And let dry for one full day before use.

You guys, when we're all together at breakfast tomorrow, I have to show you the new tricks I taught Dude. He can shake hands and play dead (which might help him if Maleficent ever comes back). He can even catch a Frisbee in midair. Ben and I were hanging out this morning, and he said everyone is really glad we stayed in Auradon, even his mom and dad.

He said he always knew we were good inside . . . and you know what? I feel like I always knew, too.

You need to bring some of that goodness out on the tourney field this afternoon! We have a rematch against the Sherwood Falcons! I want to see some of that zigzagging action that won us the game last time.

Sure, I can do that. But I've also been working on some new moves. ☺

Okay-Jay, Carlos-I know you don't like us writing about too much guy stuff in here, but

Ben is, like, my first REAL boyfriend, and that's kind of a big deal.

Tonight we're going on our first REAL date, without any spells. We might even go back to the Enchanted Lake for another picnic. It's crazy... whenever I'm around him, I feel totally at ease. There's no worrying. No plotting or trying to manipulate the situation so I'm always in control.

IT'S JUST GOOD...

... and good feels good.
Who knew, huh?

Enchanted Lake...
that reminds me, Carlos,
want to defeat Journey
into the Enchanted
Forest tonight?!?!

8 P.M.
ME & JAY'S ROOM.
BE THERE.

Hero's.
The ~~Villain's~~ Future

A villain must always look

Toward the future, keeping in

Mind her ultimate goals:

World domination, power,

Manipulation of others.

Total control.

To be hated and feared.

Fortune and infamy.

When you choose
GOODNESS,
The world comes alive again.
Life is breathed into everything you do.
Every thought, action, and desire is **PURE,**
And people shine in the light of your presence.
A HERO'S FUTURE IS ABUNDANT.
A hero cannot be stopped, no matter how
hard anyone tries.
The world opens like a flower
When you choose **good.**

How a Spell REALLY Works

So, I know I've been using this spell book and mixing potions and extracts and all that fun stuff, but after the coronation ceremony, I'm pretty sure the thing that matters most in spell casting is the **CLARITY OF YOUR INTENTION.**

The clarity of what???

Let me explain:

If you're clear in what you want and what you're doing, no one can hurt you. The mixing of the potions and the making of spelled cookies or cupcakes helps complete the spell, but it really all starts with what you're thinking and feeling. You have to **THINK CLEARLY AND FEEL STRONGLY TO COMPLETE A SPELL.**

Okay . . .
that makes a little
more sense. . . .

Glossary of Magical Terms

Alchemy: A power or process that changes or transforms something in a mysterious or impressive way.

Amulet: An ornament or small piece of jewelry that gives protection against evil, danger,

IT MAKES or disease.
TOTAL SENSE!

Like when I was staring into my mom's eyes when she was that huge, powerful dragon, the only thing that saved me was knowing, in my heart, that I was right. That her intentions weren't pure—that she wanted the wand for herself. I was thinking not only of myself, but of you guys, too, and all the people of Auradon.

I guess what I'm saying is the intention matters, and how strongly you feel matters ... but GOOD CONQUERS EVIL, too. That matters, too. I think that's the truth.

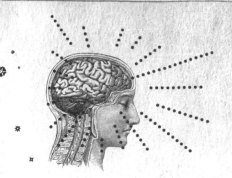

Astral projection: The act of separating the Spirit from the physical body. Also referred to as an out-of-body experience.

Aura: The distinctive atmosphere or quality that seems to surround and be generated by a person, thing, or place.

Banishment: To send or drive something away

ON THE ISLE OF THE LOST THEY SAY:
STOP! THIEF! GIVE THAT BACK!

IN AURADON THEY SAY:
SIR, PARDON ME, I THINK YOU'VE TAKEN SOMETHING THAT BELONGS TO ME.

Book of shadows: A witch's diary.

Cauldron: A large metal pot, preferably made of cast iron. A symbol of abundance.

Chant: A repeated rhythmic phrase, often used to raise energy and reach a heightened state.

Divination: Using symbols or objects to interpret messages from the Higher self.

IN AURADON THEY SAY:
OH, MY! THIS LEMONADE IS DELIGHTFUL!

ON THE ISLE OF THE LOST THEY SAY:
NOTHING. THEY YANK YOURS OUT OF YOUR HAND
AND DRINK IT.

Gem elixir: An elixir created with one or more gemstones or minerals.

Harvest moon: A full moon that is seen nearest to the time of the autumnal equinox.

Hex: A magic spell, a curse.

Meditation: The engagement in mental exercise for the purpose of reaching a heightened level of spiritual awareness.

Medium: A person who is in contact with the Spirits of the dead, and who can facilitate communication between the dead and the living.

Rootwork: The use of herbs and roots for healing and in magical practice.

Scrying: A method of divination that involves gazing into a reflective surface, such as a scrying glass, a crystal ball, or a scrying pool.

ON THE ISLE OF THE LOST THEY SAY:
What are you lookin' at? Don't make me smash your skull.

IN AURADON THEY SAY:
Oh, no... is there something in my teeth?

ON THE ISLE OF THE LOST THEY SAY:
Girl, you look like you just crawled out of a gutter.

IN AURADON THEY SAY:
I love your dress. Did you get that for the ball?

Scrying mirror: A black reflective surface, as opposed to a silver reflective one.

Smudging: Burning of herbs to purify an object, person, or area.

Scepter: An ornamental staff that may or may not have magical properties.

Spirit animal: A spirit that embodies all the characteristics of the species it represents.

ON THE ISLE OF THE LOST THEY SAY:
YOU'LL NEVER AMOUNT TO NOTHING.

IN AURADON THEY SAY:
IF YOU BELIEVE, YOU CAN ACHIEVE!

ON THE ISLE OF THE LOST THEY SAY:
I'm going to grind you into the pavement.

IN AURADON THEY SAY: Let's dance!

Talisman: An object, typically an inscribed ring or stone, that is thought to have magic powers and bring good luck.

Ward: A protection or guardian. It may be maintained by a spell, an amulet, a symbol, or some other physical or energy object.

YOU GUYS! NO MORE WORRYING ABOUT WHAT OTHERS WANT OR WHAT THEY THINK WE SHOULD BE. TIME TO WRITE OUR OWN HISTORY, OUR OWN FUTURES!

Choosing good
feels really
GOOD.

Did I just write that?!

Yes! It does!

YEAAHHH!

I AGREE.
(SO DOES DUDE.)